*Too Close
for Comfort*

**Books by
Lori Herter**

No Time for Love
Too Close for Comfort
To Have and to Hold
All Our Tomorrows
Private Screenings

*Too Close
for Comfort*

Lori Herter

SPEAKING VOLUMES, LLC
NAPLES, FLORIDA
2016

Too Close for Comfort

ISBN 978-1-62815-654-6

Chapter One

Puzzled gray eyes spotted the handwritten note lying on the table.

Jo—

Heard the fishing's great in La Paz! Leaving today, December 22. Made reservations for us at the Hotel La Playa. Left a map and guidebook so you can follow.

Baja's civilized nowadays—the new road is paved all the way. Should be a nice drive. Hope we see you by Christmas!

Dad

Joey exhaled a long sigh through soft, well-formed lips. "Well, that explains why nobody's here," Joey Scott muttered to herself as she glanced about the empty, tidied-up trailer home.

She had left Los Angeles early that morning—Christmas morning—to drive the two hundred miles to Estero

Beach, just outside Ensenada, to spend the holidays with her parents. For the past several years they had kept a mobile home in a permanent rental space at a large trailer park there, driving down often for long weekends and holidays.

Joey had intended to leave for Mexico with them five days before, but as often happened, a problem had cropped up at work which forced her to delay her departure. She had promised her parents she would drive down as soon as she could, and now that she had finally arrived, *they* were gone.

Disappointment showed on her lovely young face as her eyes moved down the sheet of paper to another note, this one written in a finer hand.

Dear Joey,
We tried to phone you, but for some reason the lines wouldn't go through to L.A. I'm sorry about this change in our plans, but you know your father. Someone who just visited La Paz told him a fish story and he can't wait to get there.

"That sounds typical," Joey mumbled, breathing out another long sigh.

I tried to tell him you shouldn't drive down there all alone to meet us, but he wouldn't pay any heed. You're so capable of looking after yourself, I think sometimes he forgets you're a girl.
Some people we met here told me that parts of Highway 1 aren't in good condition and the service stations are often out of gas, so please, dear, be careful. And don't drive at night—they say it's very dangerous. There are supposed to be some good hotels along the way, but I still don't like the idea of your

6

traveling such a long distance over barren desert alone in that little car.

Joey, if you'd rather not come, I will understand perfectly. You can notify us at the hotel if you decide against it. Please take care of yourself. Merry Christmas.

Love,
Mother

"And a Merry Christmas to you," Joey said a bit sardonically as she let the piece of paper drop back onto the table. Yes, this was just like something her father would do. He usually pleased himself first without giving a thought to anyone else. It apparently didn't occur to him that his wife and daughter might like to do something other than what he had in mind.

"It's partly Mother's fault," Joey mused as she pulled out a chair to sit down at the small table. "She's let him get away with it all these years. If he had been *my* husband . . ."

She quickly dropped the absurd thought. She would never marry anyone like her father; she had decided that long ago. It wasn't that there was a lack of affection between father and daughter. He was an engaging, energetic man, a person who could get along well with almost anyone. Joey would have been the first to acknowledge that he had provided well for her mother and had loved her all his life.

But it seemed to Joey that her mother had paid a high price for the security she enjoyed, for she had very little influence on her husband's decisions.

Still, Joey could understand her mother's acquiescence to such a dependent role throughout her twenty-five years of marriage, knowing that her mother was from a more conservative generation and was a quiet, unassertive woman as well.

Though her mother might be content with such a marriage, Josepha Scott had decided she never could. If she married at all—and in her mind that was quite a big "if"—it would have to be to a man who was ready and willing to accept a wife on a strictly equal footing. Based on her observations of her parents' marriage and her experience dealing with men in the working world, she had come to the conclusion that such a man might not exist. More to the point, she cherished the freedom she now enjoyed as a single woman living alone and felt threatened by anything or anyone she thought might curb her independence.

Breaking into her own thoughts to remind herself that she had a decision to make, she picked up the map left for her on the table. As she unfolded the paper to its fullest dimensions and scanned the long strip of land depicted on it, she was amazed, not having realized before how far Baja California extended south into the Pacific. A second glance told her that she had only been looking at the upper portion of the peninsula. Turning the long sheet of paper over, she discovered a map covering the peninsula's lower half printed on the other side. Looking toward the bottom, she noted that the location of La Paz was less than 150 miles from Cabo San Lucas, the resort town located at the very tip of the peninsula.

She began to grow uneasy about the idea of making such a long drive over an area that was notorious for its rough, and for the most part uninhabited, terrain. Scrutinizing the map more carefully, she noted that most of the larger towns were very far apart. There were a number of small villages scattered in between, but she guessed these would have few facilities for the traveler. In some areas it was a long way even between the smaller villages.

She picked up the paperback guidebook. After leafing through it for a few minutes, she grew more reassured. The book was very thorough in its descriptions of what one would find along Highway 1, the road which ran the length of the peninsula and was just recently completed by the Mexican government. Gas stations, hotels, restaurants, markets, and scenic spots were all pinpointed and described. Mention was also made of the Green Angels, a fleet of small trucks manned by bilingual mechanics whose sole purpose was to patrol the highway and aid any motoring tourists in distress.

Checking the distance table on the map, she determined it was 854 miles from Ensenada to La Paz. She estimated that if she left that afternoon, she probably could make it to her destination two days later. Glancing through the accommodations listed, she noted, as her mother had written, that there was a string of government-financed hotels along the way, built to attract tourists to the area and said to be comparable to better hotels in the United States.

Though she could anticipate many miles of dry, inhospitable desert to cross on her own, the more she read the guidebook, the less forbidding the drive to La Paz seemed. Since her only alternative was to spend her two weeks of vacation, including New Year's, alone, Joey decided there was really no reason at all why she shouldn't make the trip. "It will be good experience for me," she told herself.

Joey was at heart a cautious person and not prone to being adventurous. She continually nurtured and took pride in her growing self-reliance, however, and sought to develop an ability to cope with difficult circumstances. She wanted very much to be a woman who could stand on her own, particularly since she often felt convinced there would never be a permanent man in her life.

The drive alone down the Baja California peninsula was beginning to take on the form of a challenge—a test of her strength to deal with the unknown. She had become comfortable with, indeed had almost overcome, the problems that faced a young career woman in the business world. She decided it was time she had some new test of her ability to handle unexpected and unfamiliar situations, so that her evolving independence would have the opportunity for further development and growth.

Now she smiled at her mother's hints of danger and her thinly veiled suggestion that Joey would be better off not making the trip. It would take more than some rough road and rugged desert to scare her. And certainly, if her middle-aged father could handle the drive, there was no reason at all why she couldn't.

Chapter Two

After stocking her tiny champagne-colored hatchback with a few cans of tuna, a box of crackers, and two one-gallon bottles of purified water taken from her parents' supplies, Joey drove down the palm-lined road leading out of the well-kept trailer park.

She decided to make a quick run into Ensenada to fill her gas tank before heading south on the long journey to La Paz. Turning into a modern service station she often used when staying with her parents at Estero Beach, she pulled to a stop in front of a pump supplying unleaded gas. *"Llene el tanque, por favor,"* she told the dark-eyed Mexican attendant, using one of the few Spanish phrases she knew.

The large station was busy with several other cars filling up. Near the next island of pumps, a small group of men were standing alongside a blue van with a high, domelike top, chatting in quick, softly spoken Spanish. Casually she noted that one of the men was unusually tall for a Mexican. She also noted, with distaste, that his conversation did not hinder him from freely eyeing a shapely American

11

redhead who was getting into her car near one of the other pumps. Apparently leering males were not limited to one nationality, Joey concluded with sardonic resignation.

She got out of her car to make a fast check of her tires. As she stepped toward the back wheel, a low gust of wind made her long, tawny-blond hair flutter softly. It fell like a thick, shiny web of gossamer over her shoulders and back, the silken strands clinging to the long-sleeved black velour top she wore over rust-colored pants.

Her tall slender form moved lithely with athletic grace, this owing to her formidable weekly schedule of tennis and racketball. Her beautiful face conveyed in its natural features an impish quality, with rosy cheeks and a full, rounded mouth shaped as though it were designed for a pout. A small, upturned nose completed the mischievously angelic look. But her cool, gray eyes, with their direct and appraising gaze, gave glimpse to the keenly competent individual housed within the doll-like face and body.

The gray eyes paused in their inspection of the tires to meet the eagerly flirtatious gaze of the station attendant, who was haphazardly washing her car windows, his mind not on his work. From long experience with such situations, Joey had learned not to drop her eyes in confusion as some women might. She met his eyes directly, issuing back to him a look that was coldly polite, and unquestionably discouraging. It was the young attendant who lowered his eyes and made a more industrious effort at the windows.

The nuance of superiority in her gaze was there because the man was clearly looking upon her as an object of desire instead of as a person. To Joey, such men operated on a lower mental level than her own, and she had little patience with them. Unfortunately it often seemed to her that such men comprised the majority of the male population, a fact which never ceased to surprise and irritate her.

12

Joey was a certified public accountant for a small accounting firm, and in her work had to deal with many male clients on a professional basis. Almost invariably in each new office to which she was sent as a consultant there were at least one or two men who seemed more taken with her physical than her mental attributes. This was evidenced by the way they lingered about her desk, keeping her from her work with meaningless small talk and playful *double-entendres*. Inevitably there had been a few along the way who had wanted to be more than just playful.

Necessity had forced Joey, during her two years of experience in the working world, to develop a way of handling such men. The practised look in her eyes meant to convey to them that she regarded herself as a professional in her field, their equal, and that she had no tolerance or time for anyone who would not deal with her as such.

She was walking back toward the driver's side of her car, after ascertaining that her tires were in good shape, when she realized she was under the surveillance of another pair of admiring male eyes. These belonged to the tall man she had noticed a few minutes before, only he was alone now and leaning nonchalantly against the bright blue van.

The eyes perusing her were a warm coffee color, lustrous against his smooth brown skin and straight black hair. His rugged, angular features reflected a proud Mexican heritage, while his general bearing seemed to indicate an even disposition and easy self-confidence.

His all-encompassing gaze lingered over the sleek feminine lines of her figure, dwelling on the thick long blond locks that had fallen softly over her well-defined bosom. She colored under the uninhibited gaze that seemed to strip her of her attire, and her blush drew his candid eyes to her face.

She quickly pulled herself together and looked directly

back at him, giving him one of her most intimidating stares. The brown eyes seemed momentarily surprised, then fairly twinkled as the dark skin creased at their outer corners. His mouth formed a grin, baring strong white teeth which contrasted sharply with his dark coloring.

Joey's cool gray eyes were brought to life in a flash of anger. She gave him a scathing glare, wishing her eyes were lasers that could burn a hole through him and stop his insolent eyes. But his grin merely diminished a bit, while his gaze became more sensual, more intense. She realized with a shock that his penetrating eyes were silently issuing her an open invitation for intimacy!

Joey's expression was resolute as she quickly turned away, but her hands trembled when she pulled open her car door and darted into the driver's seat. She had slammed the door shut and started the engine when the station attendant appeared at her window asking for her payment. With unsteady fingers she extracted from her purse the right amount of brightly colored paper currency and handed it to him.

With her right hand nervously working the stickshift, her car began to jerk violently in response to the unsteady pressure of her foot on the clutch as she began to pull out of the station. After a few moments she had the car smoothly under control, and she glanced up to her rearview mirror. In the reflection she saw the tall Mexican still standing there, hands on hips, looking after her with a grin of amusement on his face and a glint sparkling in his eyes.

Within a quarter of an hour she was well out of Ensenada and driving south on Highway 1 past farmland and distant rugged hills. But Joey's mind wasn't on the scenery.

"Why did you have to get so rattled?" she asked herself aloud in the privacy of her car. "You really looked like a fool, you know that?" She stretched up to give herself an

14

upbraiding glare in the rearview mirror, then instinctively checked the road behind her, as though afraid someone were watching. The road in back was empty.

"You've run into men like him before." She continued her self-inflicted tongue lashing. "He's just like the others. Maybe more brazen, more . . . more . . . well, go ahead and say it . . . more virile. But so what? You should have been able to handle that without falling all over yourself!"

The event deeply disturbed her. She had thought she had learned to be capable of dealing calmly with all types of people. It was essential to her work that she be able to do so, as she often was required to obtain information necessary for her accounting procedures from individuals who were uncooperative, inefficient, or not as intelligent as she. She had learned to handle these situations well and had become so adept at discouraging would-be ladies' men that she no longer regarded them as a hindrance—merely a nuisance.

But what if one day one of her clients should turn out to be a man like him? The thought almost made her quake. How had he been able, without so much as one word exchanged between them, to break through her defenses so quickly, leaving her feeling shaken and vulnerable? Her mind continued to wrestle with that question for a long while.

She passed through the small agricultural community of Maneadero, where Highway 1 narrowed from a four-lane road to two lanes. As there were no shoulders provided along the pavement, the road seemed very narrow indeed. A short distance later she came to a small sign with ALTO, Spanish for stop, printed in large letters. To the right, she noticed a small, modern, brick building with windows along the front. She immediately was reminded of the instructions in her guidebook regarding the Mexican government's requirement that visitors stop at the

15

check station near Maneadero before proceeding south. Carefully she turned off the road onto the dirt and parked in front of the building.

She walked up to the Mexican official sitting behind an open window and handed him the tourist card she had obtained at the Mexican consulate in Los Angeles. She knew it was necessary that the official validate her card here, as it had not been checked earlier when she had crossed the border.

The middle-aged man in uniform carefully inspected her papers. He looked up and said something to her in Spanish which she could not understand. *"No hablo español,"* she told him.

"Birth certificate," he said in heavily accented English.

"Birth certificate?"

"Sí."

"I don't understand—*no comprendo.*"

"You must show me birth certificate."

"But I took it with me to the Mexican consulate to get the tourist card. I didn't think I'd need it here. I've never been asked for it at the border."

"Buenas tardes," a low voice interrupted. Joey turned in irritation, then froze on her feet. It was the same tall Mexican; his blue van was pulled up behind her car. He continued speaking in Spanish to the official behind the window. When they had exchanged a few words the man in uniform addressed her again.

"Do you have a passport?"

"Yes, but I didn't bring it."

A large masculine hand deftly reached into one of the little-used pockets of her dangling shoulder bag, which she had failed to rezip, and removed a small book. He placed it in her hands, amusement dancing in his brown eyes.

She blinked as she looked at her passport. How stupid of her! She had taken a four-day show tour to London a couple of months before and had forgotten to take it out of her bag when she returned.

"Oh, yes, I do have my passport," she said in her best business voice as she handed it to the official. After looking it over, he stamped her tourist card and returned both documents to her. She thanked him and then turned to the tall man standing next to her. *"Muchas gracias,"* she said with determined politeness.

"De nada," he softly responded, a bemused gleam in his eye that made Joey rage within. Twice in one day she had succeeded in making a complete idiot of herself in front of a man she didn't know and didn't want to know. The fact that he was so obviously enjoying her frustration revolted her.

He extended his right hand toward her, eyes shining, and raised his dark brows in a tentative expression. Joey wet her lips with her tongue; she would have to shake hands with him to be polite. He *had* been of assistance to her. How unsettling to have to be beholden to a man like him! Stoically she put her small hand in his. His long fingers closed securely around it, holding it captive.

He had a strong, well-formed hand, she noted. Lean and muscular, like the rest of him. It was uncalloused and the nails were trimmed and clean. He apparently did not earn his living by manual labor. Her eyes traveled along his arm, sheathed in an expensive-looking brown leather jacket, and then up to his face. He was looking at her, a curious expression in his eyes. She gently pulled her hand away.

"Adiós," she said quietly, dropping her eyes from his and turning to walk toward her car.

"Hasta luego," he called out in a nonchalant tone when she had covered the short distance to her vehicle.

She started the ignition and drove off, this time taking care to do it much more smoothly than before. *"Hasta luego . . . hasta luego . . .* what does that mean?" she mumbled under her breath when she was well away from the check station. Suddenly it came to her: See you later.

"Good Lord, I hope not," she groaned. But since he apparently was also driving along Highway 1, it seemed more than possible she could run into him again, as that road was the main thoroughfare through Baja California. "He is Mexican, though," she reminded herself. "Maybe he lives or has business in one of the towns along the way. It's unlikely he'd be driving the whole distance to La Paz. At least, I hope it's unlikely," she muttered ruefully.

Her expression suddenly changed as a new thought entered her mind. Unconsciously, her hands tightened their grip on the wheel. "If he's Mexican," she said slowly, "why was he at the check station? It's only foreign visitors that need to stop." She paled a bit. "What if . . . what if he's following me? Why else would he have stopped?" Her breathing quickened as she recalled the sensual way he had looked at her at the gas station. Did he want to make good that unspoken invitation?

"Now calm down!" she instructed herself as she pushed back into her seat. "You're getting carried away. There are many logical possibilities why he could have stopped. Maybe he knew the man behind the window. Maybe he works for the Mexican government himself and oversees the check station. And as for that look he gave you, he probably doles that out to every woman he sees," she decided, thinking of the redhead she had caught him observing. "He'd be the type who thinks he's God's gift to the female gender," she said with scorn. But her conscience silently reminded her that, judging by his appearance, the assessment might not be far from wrong. "I hate men like that!" she declared aloud, stifling the small voice within.

Glancing at her rearview mirror, she checked the empty road behind her. "You see, not a car in sight. Now concentrate on the scenery instead of that man! No doubt he thinks women are a dime a dozen, so he's not going to go out of his way to chase you!" she chided, irritated with her own obstinate tendency to overreact. It was an occasional but troublesome character flaw that she was intent on improving.

She did as she had instructed herself and began to look at the countryside. The road was winding through vineyards as she was coming into a wide, lush valley, lying peacefully between rugged, low hills.

She continued to drive through farmland interspersed with occasional small villages for almost three hours. She had gotten a late start, and it was nearing five o'clock when she came into San Quintin.

It was quite a large town strung haphazardly along the road for several miles, with many different shops and stores, cafés, banks, and mechanic's shops. It was often difficult to distinguish one business from another, for the small individual buildings of varying design did little to advertise what services were provided within. They were set rather far back from the road by American standards, and in between was barren dirt instead of sidewalks. She speculated that it must have rained quite recently, and very heavily too, for large puddles of standing water covered much of the flat land on either side of the road.

Following the instructions in her guidebook, she made her way through the town and took a right turn onto a road which led her to the hotel near the beach at which she had wanted to stay. The sun was fading quickly and it was beginning to turn chilly, so she welcomed the warmth of the lobby as she entered the modern building. She walked to the long desk and asked for a room.

"You are lucky, we do have a room left," the woman behind the desk told her in English that was not too difficult to decipher. "The road is better now and the cars can go through, so we are no longer so crowded."

"What was the problem?" Joey asked with concern.

"The heavy rains two days ago wash out the road, but today the water has gone down enough so the cars can pass," she explained.

"I see," Joey responded slowly, wondering if she had been wise to try to drive to La Paz after all. She took the key the woman gave her and, following her directions, found her room.

It was a large, beautifully furnished room with a private bath. "Not bad," she thought with a smile. She went back to the car to bring in her suitcase.

After relaxing for a while, she changed into a beige skirt and bright, multicolored blouse and walked to the hotel's small dining room. Shortly she was seated at a table near one corner of the pleasant room. It was about half full of people and several waiters strolled about. It took a while before she was presented with a menu, and she was busy perusing it when a loud, distinctly American voice distracted her.

"Hey, Mark! Over here! Well, how do you like that—small world, eh?" a man, apparently at the table behind hers, was saying boisterously.

"Hello, Ted! I didn't know you would be down here," another male American voice answered in quieter tones. Judging by the direction of the voice, he seemed to be approaching the other man's table. "Come to fish?"

"Yeah. We've been at Mulegé for a week, but coming back has been rough with these darn washouts. It wasn't bad going down."

"Where's your wife?"

"Oh, she's got a touch of Montezuma's revenge, so she's skipping dinner. She'll be okay, though. Where are you headed, Mark?"

"Cabo San Lucas."

"To pick up your old lady?"

"That's right."

Old lady! Joey cringed at the term. That any man could refer to someone's wife as his old lady seemed to her the height of disrespect.

"She's a lively little thing, isn't she?" Ted, who sounded older than the other man, commented.

"That she is," the younger, quieter voice answered with a nuance of pride.

"With her to take care of you, Mark, I can see why you haven't bothered getting married."

This was becoming more intriguing by the second. Apparently the woman in question wasn't even the younger man's wife!

"I live by myself, Ted," she heard the quiet voice respond with a chuckle.

"She must be just a part-time old lady," thought Joey sarcastically. Curiosity was getting the better of her. She had to see what sort of men would talk over such personal matters so openly in a restaurant. Cautiously she turned around.

"*Buenas tardes,*" the tall, black-haired man said, his lustrous brown eyes already on her. Dressed in a shirt, white pullover sweater, and tan pants, he was standing by the table behind hers where a middle-aged man was seated.

Joey was stunned. It was the same Mexican she had met on the road. But he was an American! He must have thought it a joke at the check station when he had let her believe he was a local. She gave him a very abbreviated nod of recognition and stiffly turned back to face her table again, anger making her stomach churn.

"Well, Mark, I was just about to get up and leave," the older man said with more enthusiasm than the statement

21

required. "Great to see you again." Then he added in a lower, conspiratorial tone, "Good luck *fishing.*" This was immediately followed by a throaty, between-us-boys laugh.

"Okay, Ted," the tall man answered calmly. "See you later."

After a moment Joey heard a few footsteps coming toward her. "Mind if I sit down?" Mark asked, resting a hand on the high back of her chair.

"Yes," she said, turning her face upward to meet his gaze.

The dark eyes widened and a slow smile crossed his face. "Mind if I ask why?"

"I prefer to eat alone," she responded coolly, facing forward again.

Casually he moved to the chair opposite hers on the other side of the table and, stooping slightly, leaned with folded arms over the chair's back. "Here we are," he said with a poetic gesture of his hand, "two Americans meeting by chance in a foreign land, and you don't even want to talk to me?"

"This hotel seems to be full of Americans. Besides, I thought you were Mexican," she replied, an insinuating tone in her voice.

"I am—Mexican descent. And because I speak fluent Spanish, you assumed I was born south of the border. If you had checked, you would have seen my California license plate."

Joey realized she had been too busy looking at the man to pay much attention to his vehicle. "You knew *I* was American. You could have spoken to me in English at the check station," she countered.

"That would have been too easy," he responded with a grin.

22

"Do you enjoy amusing yourself at the expense of others?" she asked querulously.

"Sure—especially when they get huffy about it. Now, I might remind you that if I hadn't intervened, you might not be sitting here right now. And since this dining room is beginning to get crowded, I suggest it would be polite if you asked me to join you."

Joey swallowed and lowered her eyes from his expectant gaze. "Go ahead and sit down," she murmured grudgingly. She might have known he would take advantage of the favor he had done her.

"So kind of you to ask me," he joked, taking the seat opposite her. He leaned back in the chair and tilted his head to one side. "Tell me, why do you dislike me so much? We don't even know each other."

The directness of his question took her unexpectedly. "I . . . I just don't like your type, that's all."

"I'm a type?" he asked with surprise. "What type am I?"

"A womanizer—a man with no respect or sensitivity toward women," she said nervously, hoping to discourage his pursuit by bluntly telling him what she thought of him.

"Really! And how have you come to that conclusion?"

She hesitated. The conversation she had just overheard would have proven her point, but she didn't want to appear an eavesdropper. "The way you looked me over in Ensenada," she replied, trying not to appear embarrassed, though she felt the color rising in her cheeks.

"A man admiring a beautiful woman. Is there something wrong with that?" he said calmly, staring at her.

Joey was beginning to feel skittish under his eyes, but she went on boldly. "You were admiring a face and body. It wouldn't have interested you to find out what kind of person I was."

"Since I had never met you, what else was I supposed

to admire? And I'm trying very hard now to figure out what kind of a person you are."

Did he have to be so adept at sparring with her? She longed to confront him with that blatantly sensual invitation he had silently given her, but she found herself incapable of expressing it aloud—at least to him. Even now there was a certain look in his eyes as he softly added, "You seem to have assumed a lot about me in the few brief moments we've been together."

Been together. For some reason, the words made Joey's heart beat faster. Why did everything he did and say seem so suggestive?

"I just don't like being treated like a . . . sex object," she said defensively. It was with great difficulty she uttered the last words to him, but she managed, regaining some pride in having at least made clear her point of view.

It appeared he would have answered her, but before he could, a waiter arrived at their table to take their orders. Joey quickly named the first thing listed on the menu. She hadn't had an opportunity to make up her mind, but wanted to appear as though she were in total control of herself.

Mark gave his order and asked for a bottle of wine for them to share. She looked up at him abruptly; she had no wish to make an occasion of this meal. But he merely met her eyes with a steady, affable gaze, quelling her unspoken objection.

"What's your name?" he asked in a friendly tone when the waiter had gone. He apparently wanted to drop their previous topic and start anew.

"Josepha Scott."

"Josepha . . ." he pondered. "I would have guessed your name to be Cindy or Sally . . . or Barbie."

"I'm not a doll," she stated matter-of-factly.

"You look like one," he countered with a smile. "Don't you have a nickname or something?"

"My father and some of my co-workers call me Jo. Others call me Joey."

His smile broadened. "Joey . . . that's adorable. It suits you. But how did your parents come to name you Josepha?"

"I was their first and only child. My father had wanted a boy, but unfortunately he couldn't control nature and had to make do with a daughter. They had planned to name me Joseph, after a relative, so they made it Josepha instead."

"I may be mistaken, but it sounds like you aren't too fond of your father."

She smiled slightly. "Oh, I am. He's a well-meaning person. It's just that he has a tendency to think women are around to cater to his wishes. One has to be a man to gain his true respect."

"I see. Another insensitive male?"

"I suppose you might say that."

"You seem to get more than your share of them."

"It often strikes me that way," she readily agreed.

The conversation died of its own accord for a few moments.

"You haven't asked what *my* name is," he said, breaking the stiff silence.

"No, I haven't," Joey replied smoothly, implying the neglect was intentional.

He smiled. "I'm Mark Chavira." As there was no comment, he added, "I live in Orange County. I'm in real estate development." There was still no response from the beautiful mannequinlike creature sitting across from him. "What do *you* do?" he finally asked.

"I work for the Layton and Brook Accountancy Corporation in Los Angeles. I'm a certified public accountant," she told him, quietly anticipating the response she often received from men upon hearing this revelation. She was not disappointed; the dark brown eyes widened. True to form, she assumed, he was surprised that an attractive young woman could also be a competent businessperson. But an instant later he startled her by smiling cordially while his eyes became infused with admiration.

"I have great regard for those in your profession." The tone of his voice reflected his sincerity. "Without accountants to assist me in my work, my records would be a shambles and investors wouldn't have much faith in me."

This statement left Joey at a loss. In her experience men often preferred to ignore her business status or they gave her a tolerant respect. The generosity of this man's statement threw her. Suddenly feeling strangely shy, she dropped her eyes to the wineglass that had been placed in front of her.

"My expertise lies in finding good tracts of land and putting the right buildings on them," he continued. "I back away when it comes to the details involved in keeping records in order and accounts balanced. I'm one of those who can see the forest clearly, but the trees are blurred," he said with a chuckle.

This artless confession confused Joey more. She was not used to hearing a man so readily point out his weaknesses, especially to a woman. In fact, she herself would not be willing to openly admit her shortcomings. She had always thought it advantageous to appear proficient in all things.

Her curiosity aroused, she drew him out over dinner in what unexpectedly turned into a pleasant conversation. From what he told her about his work, she deduced that he must be quite successful. Though he did not boast, the passing mention of shopping centers and office buildings that his organization had developed indicated his was no small-time operation.

Joey was eager to learn more, but as their empty plates were removed, he said amiably, "Enough of this business talk. Tell me about yourself. How is it you're driving alone through Baja California on Christmas Day?"

"I'm going down to join my parents. We were to spend the holidays at Estero Beach, but my father changed his mind. They left a note saying I should meet them in La Paz."

Mark looked concerned. "Your father wanted you to drive all that way alone? Has he ever driven to La Paz himself?"

"No, I don't think so. Why?"

He shook his head. "It's a long, lonely trip through an empty, isolated desert. The terrain is rough and the road is full of potholes. Your father must not have realized what the area is like, because I don't think any man would want his daughter to make the trip alone."

"Well, my father often does minimize obstacles, but if others drive down there, there's no reason I shouldn't," she said, holding her chin a bit higher. "You're driving alone, aren't you?"

"Yes," he agreed, "but I know the area from many previous trips, and I'm self-contained in my van. If I can't get a hotel room, as I couldn't tonight, or I'm not near a restaurant, I always have food and shelter with me. Besides . . . a young woman traveling alone . . ." He left off, shaking his head.

Joey's confidence was undermined a bit by these remarks, but she would not allow herself to be set back. She decided to attack his weakest point.

"I don't see what difference it should make that I'm female. Besides, I stocked some provisions and I could sleep in my car if I had to."

The concern came back into his eyes. "I have to admire your g . . . intestinal fortitude, but your courage may be foolhardy. Baja California is no place for a woman alone. One runs into all sorts of people along Highway 1, not all of them trustworthy. If you should get stranded, you could find yourself in quite a predicament. And the problem would be compounded by the fact that you don't know much Spanish. Not many of the local people in this area speak English."

"I still don't see what my being a woman has to do with it," she retorted stubbornly, blithely overlooking his other arguments.

He grinned. "I take it you're very equality-minded. I appreciate your feelings, but I'm afraid I'll have to maintain my point of view. While women can and do function just as well as men in a modern metropolis, it's a different story when it comes to surviving in a rugged, unimproved area. I think you must agree that women are physically weaker than men. That's probably why women in less civilized times were willing to accept male protection. You must remember, Joey, that traveling through Baja California, with the exception of its few larger cities, is somewhat like going back in time a hundred years or more. Everything may be fine as long as you don't run into any problems, but I don't like to think what might happen to you. if you lost what little protection your automobile provides."

Joey swallowed hard, as if physically trying to keep her fears from rising up and overwhelming her. She allowed resentment to take over. "My first impression of you was correct. You seem to think of a woman as merely a helpless, cute little toy. You probably can't even fathom the notion that we are intelligent and resourceful individuals. Not every obstacle is overcome by muscle power. We may cope with a tough situation differently than a man would, but we still cope!"

He took his napkin and casually threw it next to his

empty coffee cup. "I didn't intend to start an argument with you, Joey, and I do admire your courage. Just be careful on the road, okay?" he said with a conciliatory smile.

She nodded her head slightly in agreement, dropping her eyes to the table, for she was already beginning to feel dissatisfied with herself about sounding so obstinate. Even if she didn't like him or his attitudes, there was no reason to let herself become antagonized, she reasoned. Why should his opinions be of any consequence to her?

The waiter brought the check and handed it to Chavira. Joey saw Mark begin to reach for his wallet and hurried to say, "I'll pay for my own," as she reached to the floor for her shoulderbag.

"Pay for your own! No, no, I'll get it," he said with a smile.

"No, really, I insist. I always pay my own way," she said, taking out her own wallet.

"Now, I can't believe that. As a CPA, you must allow your clients to take you out to lunch."

"Of course, just as I often take them to lunch at our company's expense. But you aren't one of my clients. In nonbusiness matters, I prefer separate checks. It keeps things simpler." Besides, she added to herself, I don't want to owe you any more favors.

He kept an amused and thoughtful silence for a moment. "I don't see that anything's so complicated. Why not let me pay for this, and you can pick up the tab next time? It would all work out evenly in the end and save us the chore of dividing the bill."

Joey tried to keep her patience. "Next time? I don't foresee any next time, Mr. Chavira. And as for dividing the check, it's no chore for me. I'll be happy to do the arithmetic."

He leaned back in his chair, still holding the wallet in

his hand, and studied her with interest. "I don't think I've ever met a woman quite so determined as you are to have her way," he said, a hint of admiration in his eyes.

"Now you have," she stated a little smugly. She reached over and turned the bill toward her so that she could read it. "Let's see . . ." she muttered as she began to figure her portion of the total.

Suddenly it was snatched up from under her eyes. "I'm afraid I can be equally determined, Miss Scott. I'm paying the check," he said as he rose from his chair.

Quickly she got up to intercept him. "Why won't you honor my wishes in this?" she demanded.

He put his hands on his hips and looked down into her unyielding, upturned face, taking a step closer. Humor played in his eyes as he said, "Why, Joey? Let's say because I'm bigger than you, so I can do as I please. Do you think you can stop me?" He raised his brows and waited for her answer.

Anger sparked in her eyes and a few choice retorts rose to her lips. She kept herself from uttering them. He was obviously baiting her; why give him the satisfaction of seeing that he had managed to rouse her temper? Abruptly she turned away from him and coolly stalked out of his presence, walking between tables toward the door.

Once out in the lobby of the hotel she quickened her stride and headed toward the hallway down which her room was located. Of all the domineering, pigheaded, overbearing men! she fumed, angrily jerking her key out of her bag.

She heard quick footsteps coming up behind her. "Joey, wait!" Mark was beside her now, looking down at her tight-lipped profile. "I'm sorry if I've offended you, but you were so stubborn I couldn't resist giving you a little set-down. After your claims that you can cope with anything, I thought for your own good you should be made aware that you're not quite invincible."

"So you've proved your point," she said icily, looking straight ahead and continuing her fast pace. "Would you please leave me alone now?"

He bowed his head for a moment, but kept up with her. "Look, I . . . was wrong. I shouldn't have made you angry like this. I'm sorry. But I do think you were making a mountain out of a molehill about paying the check," he persisted.

Immediately she stopped in the middle of the long, narrow hallway and faced him. "I feel I have every right to choose who I keep company with and who I'll allow to take me to dinner! I have no respect for skirt chasers who foist their unwelcome attentions on me."

"Womanizer! Skirt chaser!" he exclaimed, continuing beside her as she resumed her pace. "How do you know I'm those things?"

She suddenly stopped again, realizing she had passed her room. She turned and retraced a few steps until she came to her door.

"It's not really very hard," she said, holding the key poised by the doorknob as he came up to her. "I remember the way you leered at me in Ensenada, only minutes after you had finished similarly eyeing a redhead who was at the same gas station. Why else would you have insisted on joining me for dinner? It doesn't take much insight to see that you're after me."

"The redhead," he murmured thoughtfully, leaning casually against the doorframe. "You're very observant. I would never have remembered." He smiled a little. "So you think the reason I bought you dinner was to try to make time with you."

"Why else?" she asked flatly, looking up at him. At last

31

she felt she was gaining the upper hand. In another moment or two she would be rid of him.

"Indeed—why else?" he replied. An unsettling light entered his eye as he looked over her face. He drew himself away from the wall in an easy movement and stood erect in front of her. "Well . . . I certainly wouldn't want to spoil your image of me," he said in a soft, smooth, voice. He moved closer and very calmly placed his hands at her waist. "Particularly when you're so sure you're right." He pulled her closer and his eyes settled sensually on her soft mouth. Panic showed clearly on Joey's face as she pressed her hands against his chest, vainly trying to push herself out of his grasp. "Relax, Joey, this will be over in a minute."

He pulled her up against him and pressed his lips to hers. She could feel his warm breath against her cheek as his arms enclosed her. Locked in his strong embrace, it seemed to Joey that he took every last second of his minute before he finally let her go.

After taking a moment to recapture her breath and her wits, she cried with wrath, "You are the rudest man I have ever met!"

He put his hands on his hips and quietly laughed. "That's quite a distinction! Since I'll have such an important place in your memory, I'll have to give you another chance to savor my revolting personality." He took the key from her hand and turned to unlock her door. "I'll pick you up for breakfast at seven thirty tomorrow," he said as he dangled the key in front of her.

She snatched it out of his long fingers. "I don't want to see you at breakfast, or ever again!"

He smiled broadly, bemusement making his eyes sparkle. Leaning toward her he said, "Good night, Joey. Merry Christmas!" then turned and took a few steps down the hall. He stopped briefly to call back to her, "Remember—seven thirty!"

Joey hurried into her room, slamming the door behind her. "What a horrible man!" she rasped as she threw down her shoulderbag and key onto the dresser. "Rude, domineering, presumptuous . . . strong." Suddenly the sensation of being locked in his arms swept over her again. She stood as if in a trance in the middle of the room, her arms crossed tightly over her chest and her long hair cascading over her slender shoulders, while a multitude of contradictory thoughts and feelings rushed through her. In the course of a day he had made her suspect, fear, and dislike him. But his kiss had been curiously gentle as he had kept her pressed firmly against him. The memory of it warmed and comforted her until suddenly she realized she was on the verge of tears.

Shaking her head sharply, she tried to rid herself of the lump in her throat. "I'm not afraid, I'm not lonely, and I don't need a man to make me happy!" she recited through clenched teeth. "Particularly not *that* man!"

Her expression became resolute. "Sorry to spoil your plans for breakfast, Mr. Chavira, but I won't be here at seven thirty tomorrow morning," she said as she began undressing with a vengeance, throwing her clothes onto the bed. She raced into the bathroom, took a shower, brushed her teeth, and put on her nightgown.

Realizing she had not brought along her travel alarm, she searched about the room for the telephone. There was none. "I can't even get a wake-up call!" she muttered in frustration. "Well, there's no need," she assured herself. "I always wake up when I want to anyway. And tomorrow," she told herself with a smug smile, "I'm getting up at six thirty and I'll be on the road by seven!" She fell asleep to the pleasant image of Mark Chavira knocking at the door of her empty room.

Chapter Three

Joey awakened suddenly, opening startled eyes as she lifted her head from the pillow. A loud rapping sound quickly brought her to a sitting position.

"Joey, it's seven thirty! You up?" she heard Mark Chavira's voice from the outer hall.

"Oh, no," she groaned. Realizing her plans were ruined, she quickly put her mind in gear. "If I don't answer, maybe he'll think I've left," she silently reasoned, stiffening her body to ensure no sound would give her presence away.

"Your car is still outside, Joey, so I know you're in there," came his teasing voice.

Stifling an oath, she threw aside the covers and grabbed her long navy blue robe, tying the belt as she hurried to the door.

"Well, good morning!" Chavira crowed with disgusting good cheer when she had opened the door. Noting her peevish expression, he asked in solicitous tones, "Did I wake you up?" while a mocking smile betrayed his amusement at her sleepy eyes and rumpled hair.

"I don't have my travel alarm and there's no phone in the room," she explained impatiently.

"You might have slept til noon, if you didn't have me around. Aren't you grateful?" he asked, eyes twinkling.

"Eternally. It will take me a while to get dressed, so why don't you just go ahead and have breakfast. . . ."

"You should know by now you can't get rid of me that easily. I'll wait for you in the lobby," he said good-naturedly.

He made no move to go, however. His attention was drawn to her attire, particularly the ruffles of her white flannel nightgown, accented by small, decorative ribbons, which peeked out from under her robe at her throat, wrists, and over her bare toes.

"Something wrong?" she asked, pulling the robe closer about her.

He leaned lazily against the doorframe. "I just happened to be wondering late last night what a modern, independent young woman like yourself wears to bed."

"I'm surprised you don't already know," she answered, affecting a tone of impatient indifference.

"It was quite an interesting problem," he continued, unperturbed. "I decided that either she would wear pajamas like a man, to symbolize her equality, or she would put on a flimsy black negligee to prove herself unfettered by the old restrictive moral code. But here you are, Joey, covered from neck to toe in pure white flannel and little pink bows, the image of Victorian innocence."

Joey cast her eyes downward in uneasy silence.

"It isn't that I disapprove," he continued in a soft voice. "I think you look charming. In fact, it's what I would have expected after that kiss last night."

Her apprehensive gray eyes flicked up to his momentarily before lowering again to the floor. Clasping the knob

35

unsteadily, she began to close the door, murmuring, "I'll be ready in a few minutes."

She heard him softly reply, "I'll be waiting," before she shut him out. A trembling hand went to her forehead, as if to remove him from her mind as well. His incisive comments were unnerving, as if he possessed some secret magnifying glass with which he could see through the thick armor of protective self-reliance she worked so hard to keep in place. His uncanny intuition shook her deeply.

She had regained a tenuous control over her nerves by the time she had left her room to meet him in the lobby. She was dressed in casual green pants and a matching sweater, her hair hurriedly but neatly brushed into place. It was chilly and she shivered a bit as she approached him.

"You'd better wear a jacket when you go out; it's pretty cold this morning," he admonished her.

Joey nodded in response. They walked into the dining room and sat down at a table. Before long their orders were taken and they were left together in uneasy silence.

"Where did you stay last night?" she ventured, finding the silence too nerveracking.

"There's a trailer park near here, so I pulled in and slept in my van. The place had nice facilities, but the hot water wasn't working. Taking a cold shower in these temperatures isn't much fun."

"I didn't have any hot water either, but at least the room was heated," she said with a smile.

"That's some consolation. How far are you planning to drive today?"

"Guerrero Negro or San Ignacio."

"That's pretty ambitious for the shape the road is in. They've had some washouts south of here, you know."

"I didn't get as far as I had hoped to yesterday. Even if I make it to San Ignacio, I'll still be behind schedule."

"Your parents are expecting you by a certain time?"

36

"No, but they may begin to wonder where I am. And the sooner I get there, the more time I'll have to spend with them," she explained.

"I understand, but you'll make it to Guerrero Negro today only if you're very lucky. Don't be tempted to drive at night. It's very dangerous, did you know that?"

"I remember reading that in my guidebook. Something about cattle on the road?"

"Yes, they often wander onto the asphalt at night for warmth. Many are black or brown, so they're hard to see in the dark. If you ran into one, both your car and the cow could be demolished."

"I'll try to avoid night driving then."

"Don't even consider it!" he corrected firmly.

There's no need to be so domineering about it, she silently grumbled. Their breakfast plates were brought, and as they dug into scrambled eggs and bacon, Mark abruptly changed the subject.

"How long have you been working for Layton and Brook?"

Surprised that he had remembered the name of her company, she replied, "For two years—since I graduated from college."

"That makes you about twenty-four, then?"

"Yes," she answered, a little piqued that he had asked the question merely to ascertain her age. "How old are you?"

"Thirty-three. I suppose you passed your CPA exam on the first try."

"Yes," she replied, caught off guard again.

"You're such a determined young woman, I thought that would be the case. Was it a surprise to any of the male students in your class?"

"I don't know. Since I always got better grades than

37

most of them, they didn't hang around me much," she said with some asperity.

"Well, it could be a blow to some young men to be outdone by a cute little chick—you'll pardon the expression," he said, smiling with the apology. "You must have had a boyfriend though."

Joey's expression became guarded. "Yes," she said, staring at her plate.

Her reaction seemed to kindle Mark's interest. "Was it serious?" he asked quietly.

Joey's lips formed a brittle smile. "I thought it was. Apparently he didn't."

"What happened—did he walk out on you?"

"He wasn't honest enough to do anything as straightforward as that," she said, a tenseness hardening her eyes. "I discovered him with my roommate one day. They were . . . in a rather compromising pose. Even then he tried to cover it over with lame excuses. So I walked out on *him.*" Her voice unintentionally revealed her bitterness.

"Poor Joey," Mark said, his attention focused on the hurt in her eyes that her tautly composed expression could not conceal. "No wonder you have a low opinion of men."

"My opinion of men is based on more than just that," Joey retorted defensively. "I don't like . . ."

"Hey, Mark! Thought I might run into you this morning." It was Ted, the gray-haired man with baggy eyes that Mark had spoken with the night before. Joey had been too distracted even to notice him approach.

"Hello, Ted," Mark said, rising up a bit to shake hands.

"Well, I see you did have some luck . . ." the older man quipped, with a long glance toward Joey, ". . . fishing, that is." He directed a sly look to Mark.

"Ted, this is Joey Scott," Mark hurried to say. "She's a CPA for a firm in Los Angeles."

"Oh, you don't say." Ted responded, somewhat discomfited. Recovering, he threw in, "Prettiest little CPA *I* ever saw!"

"This is Ted Morley," Mark plunged on with the introductions."He's one of my investors."

Joey nodded briefly.

"I didn't realize you two were . . . ah . . . business associates. Traveling together to Cabo San Lucas to work on your investment project?" Ted asked Mark, all innocence.

"No, no," Mark made haste to reply, directing an uneasy glance at Joey. "We happened to become acquainted on the road and then ran into each other again last night at dinner. I invited Joey to meet me for breakfast this morning," he explained. "Is your wife still sick?" he asked as if trying to deflect the other man's train of thought.

"No, she seems to be all right. I just came on ahead to get a table. You know how women are—always fussing with their hair and one thing or another. I got tired of waiting. Besides, the scenery's better here," he said, giving Joey a sidelong look. "Now if my wife would come out looking like this little lady, I wouldn't mind waiting around." He lifted his eyes toward the doorway. "Oh, here she is now. I'd better get back before she finds something to complain about. See you around, Mark. Nice to meet you, Miss . . . ah . . . ."

"Scott," Joey supplied.

"So long, Ted," Mark said, showing a touch of relief.

"One of your friends?" Joey asked glacially.

"I'm sure you have to deal with all types of people in your job, just as I do," he said without apology. "Ted has money, but not much tact. He's a good businessman, though—owns a small chain of drugstores."

Their waiter came by and, after clearing away their empty plates, placed the check on the table. Joey eyed the slip of paper, but made no move to pick it up. She raised her gaze to Mark, who was looking at her expectantly. "I don't suppose you'd let me pay for my own," she said tersely.

He grinned. "Just to prove how gallant I can be, I'll let you pay the whole thing, if you'd like."

Somehow she had to smile. "Thank you," she said with humorous sarcasm as she reached to pick up the bill.

In a few minutes they were walking down the hall to her room, engaged in an innocuous conversation about the weather. When they reached her door, Mark drew up in front of her in his languid way and said, "Thank you for breakfast, Miss Scott. Please allow me to repay your kindness." In an instant his arms had closed about her and he lowered his slightly smiling mouth toward hers.

"No!" she whispered, her lips brushing his as she twisted her head away. His kiss landed on her cheek.

"What's the matter, Joey?" came his gentle, low voice in her ear as he continued to hold her close. "Did you enjoy it too much last night? I know I did." The firm hands at her back pressed her tighter against his chest.

"I didn't like it in the least!" she stormed, wriggling out of his grasp. "You are the most conceited, loathsome . . ."

"I'm flattered you find me such a colorful character," he exclaimed with provoking good humor.

Snatching her key from her bag with an angry hand, she said harshly, "I hope I never have to set eyes on you again!"

"Since we're both traveling in the same direction, it's very likely we *will* see each other again," he said with an assured smile.

"Then I hope you'll find the decency to leave me alone!" she told him vehemently before entering her room and slamming the door in his face.

Within half an hour Joey was back on the road, driving

past cultivated green fields interspersed by areas of natural desert growth. The sky was overcast, and as the road followed the coastline the gray Pacific Ocean was barely in sight to the west. Occasionally she would pass a few small homes scattered haphazardly a little distance from the highway, some made of gray cement, some of stucco and brightly painted, while others were precariously constructed of wood scraps and left bare. Clotheslines of colorful wash radiated from the houses, while dogs roamed about aimlessly or lay dozing nearby on the ground.

Joey's mind was too preoccupied to pay more than intermittant attention to the passing countryside, however. Again Mark Chavira had somehow managed to come close to her vulnerable core, leaving her nervous system unbalanced. Now he had probed into her past, discovering there the lingering hurt she had hoped she'd forgotten. Though she hadn't thought of it for many months, she realized the wrenching memory of her shattered romance was with her still.

But what was Mark Chavira about that he seemed so intent on dissecting her personality? Why should he care whether she liked her father, what had happened to break up an old romance, or that she wore an old-fashioned nightgown to bed? His prying was too close for comfort.

Her complete attention was drawn back to the highway suddenly, when she realized she was approaching a standing pool of muddy water which completely covered a portion of the road just ahead. The water was contained in a low spot on the road, but its expanse was greater than the length of her car. It was difficult to estimate how deep it was. She drove almost to the water's edge and stopped. There were no other cars in sight.

Pondering the situation for a moment, she decided there was nothing to do but forge ahead. Slowly she moved her car forward. Beneath the water the pavement felt secure, if a little bumpy, and she saw that the pool was not so deep after all. Soon she was through it and back on dry road again. Pleased with herself, she breathed a relaxed sigh and pushed her foot on the accelerator to regain her previous speed.

She passed through two more small washouts before coming into a town next to a wide river valley. Noting her gas tank was little more than half full, she pulled into a service station. The attendant began filling her tank with unleaded gas as she requested, but in a few minutes he came back to her car window and told her in mixed Spanish and English that the pump had run out of gas. She had gotten only about two gallons. She paid the attendant and drove out of the town, making a mental note to stop at the next station she saw.

The road turned east and inland outside of town, and Joey drove on past scrubby vegetation and low, eroded hills in the distance. Soon she noticed a number of cars, campers, and trucks, most of them American, had pulled off the pavement, and ahead was a bottleneck of vehicles in the road. Beyond that she caught a glimpse of another expanse of water and mud. She pulled off of the road and parked her car in the sandy dirt.

After getting out and locking up her car, she walked alongside the road toward the washout to get a better look at the situation. When she got closer, she was struck by the immense size of the washout, but then saw what the real problem was. A yellow van coming from the other direction, muddy water lapping over its California license plate, was sitting almost at right angles across the inundated road. Pulling behind it, a huge mobile home had become stuck at a precarious angle in soft mud alongside the pavement.

She guessed the driver had thought it better to go off the road to avoid the submerged stretch of pavement, not realizing his heavy trailer would quickly sink into the sandy mire. He apparently had tried to turn back onto the pavement again, but his sinking trailer had held him fast. Thus the road was virtually blocked until the van and its trailer could be moved.

Joey was wondering how long a delay was in store when she felt a hand at her back and heard a low voice say, "I told you we'd meet again."

"Oh, no," Joey sighed inwardly. She turned toward Mark briefly, saying, "So we have," then abruptly hastened back toward her car. She was conscious of quick, solid footsteps gaining on her.

"Where are you off to in such a hurry?" he was asking an instant later when he had caught up with her.

"Back to my car."

"Planning on going somewhere?"

At once she realized how silly she looked. The only place she could go was back where she came from. She slowed her pace, trying to cover her frustration at her inability to deal with Mark in any sort of poised manner. "Do you suppose it will be a long delay?" she asked in an even voice.

"I expect it will," he replied. "It looks to me like they'll have to bring in special equipment to pull that heavy trailer out of the mud. No telling how long that'll take."

Joey was dismayed. "I wanted to make it to Guerrero Negro by tonight," she said in a worried tone.

"Don't count on it." They walked on in silence for a few paces. "Since we'll be stuck here for a while, why don't we go back to my van? We could play cards—have some sandwiches."

To be alone with Mark Chavira in a van was about the last thing Joey would choose to do. "No, thanks," she said sharply.

By this time they had reached her car. As she unlocked her door, he said, "You'd rather sit here by yourself?"

"Yes," she replied in a challenging undertone.

His dark eyes turned cool as he regarded her intently. "You still don't like me, do you?"

"No, Mr. Chavira, I don't. And I wish you would do as I asked earlier and leave me alone!"

She saw his jaw muscles tighten. "All right, Joey. Any way you want it. I wish you luck," he replied in a softly controlled voice.

She got into her car and firmly shut the door. "He doesn't take rejection very well," she gloated waspishly. But her attempted laugh caught in her throat as through the car window she watched him walk away from her, a tall paragon of masculinity, pride showing in each long, firm stride. Should a sudden earthquake shake the ground beneath him, she knew it would never jar his calm assurance.

She sensed an odd, unfamiliar feeling within, pulling her spirits down as she watched him stop to chat with a young couple standing next to the car just behind his parked van. She found herself wondering what he was saying, noting how easily he made conversation with strangers, for already the three were laughing together. She bowed her head, her eyes settling on her slender fingers idly resting on the bottom of the steering wheel. Maybe she should apologize. . . .

Sharp knocking on her side window brought her to attention. She turned to her left and saw two faces peering in at her. As she lowered the window halfway, she took the opportunity to study them more carefully.

They appeared to be young men in their twenties, unshaven, and dressed in old blue jeans and jackets. After her window was open, she detected the faint smell of liquor.

"Hey, you travelin' alone?" one of them asked, his hand wrapped around a paper cup, whose contents looked about to spill.

Joey sensed it was best not to answer that question. "Was there something you wanted?" she asked in a short tone of voice.

The young American seemed to find her answer amusing and slithered a glance to his companion. Returning his eyes to her, he said, "My friend and I have some Margarita mix and lots of good tequila. We thought maybe you'd like to join us. Our pick-up truck is just across the road . . ." He moved aside a bit to clear her view.

"No, thanks."

"Oh, come on! You'll get bored sittin' here all by yourself. Why not join us? Have some fun."

"I said no, thanks!"

"Look, you don't have to get snooty about it. My friend and I saw you sittin' here lookin' kinda lonely. We figured we'd be neighborly and invite you over. You're a foxy lookin' lady. Why don't you try bein' a little more sociable?" Suddenly he had opened her car door. "Hey, the rest of you is even better," he said, a glint forming in his eye. "Come on!" He reached in to grab her arm. "Just one friendly drink, huh?"

Joey quickly reached for her bag and pushed herself past them out of the car. She began walking in fast, determined paces up the road.

"Hey, where're you goin'?" he said as the two fell in step behind her.

Joey kept walking, her eyes on Mark, whose back was to her while he continued to talk with the young couple. As she moved toward him, he drew away from them and began to walk toward his van. She quickened her pace.

"Mark," she called just as he was about to open the door to the driver's side.

He turned, a warm smile brightening his face when he saw her coming to him. The smile faded as he noted her agitated expression. "What's wrong?" He raised his eyes to the two men following and instantly knew. His eyes became like brown flint and his mouth a grim line as he stared at them. The hardness of his expression frightened her a bit, though the hands which had reached to grasp her arms remained gentle.

"Look, man, we thought she was alone," she heard the one who had done all the talking explain. Mark pulled her toward him and continued to stare at them over the top of her head. "Hey, no harm done, huh? We'll uh . . . be on our way." Footsteps in the sandy dirt behind her indicated they were walking off toward their truck.

Joey breathed a bit easier while Mark let go of her. As he leaned up against his van and folded his arms over his chest, she became aware that his stern regard was now directed toward her. Not daring to look up, she whispered, "Go ahead and say it."

"All right. You didn't want my company, but you came running to me the minute you were in trouble. When I saw you coming, I thought perhaps you wanted to . . . be friends."

"Apologize," she corrected. "I should have come to apologize. I was thinking about it when those men came over."

"Thinking about it?" he said with a smile. "And would you have come if they hadn't bothered you?"

Joey hesitated. "I don't know," she answered sheepishly.

He softly chuckled. "Well, at least you're honest. I'm glad you came to me, whatever the reason, Joey." He reached out a hand and took her by the elbow. "How about a sandwich? No strings attached," he offered, a gleam of amusement in his eye.

"Thanks," she replied, smiling.

Mark led Joey around the van to the side facing away from the road and pulled open the large sliding door at the center of the long vehicle. Two steps up and she was standing on soft, plush, dark blue carpeting. Opposite the sliding door were dark wood cabinets and a tiny stainless steel sink with a pump faucet. Across the back of the van was a long upholstered seat which she guessed could double as a bed. In front of the small couch was a tiny table, and there were curtained windows above and to either side of it. The high dome top enabled them to stand erect inside without worry of hitting their heads.

"This is very nice," she said, sincerely admiring the spotless, compact vehicle.

"Thank you!" he replied with enthusiasm. "That's the first compliment you've ever given me. Would you like to sit in back or up front?"

"Oh, the front I think," she replied, eyeing the comfortable-looking high-back passenger seat. "That way we can keep track of any progress they make on the stuck trailer."

"So far they haven't gotten anywhere. They can't seem to disengage the trailer from the van, probably because the trailer's tilted at such an angle. It may have bent something out of shape," he explained. "Would you like a beer?"

"That sounds good," she said as she moved toward the brown leather passenger seat. "Oh, it swivels!" she said brightly, sitting down and proceeding to turn herself about, much as any five-year-old would.

"Are you sure you're old enough to have this?" he said, extending to her a filled plastic glass and half-full bottle of beer.

"Yes," she replied, a little embarrassed at her own lapse of decorum. "Oh, I couldn't drink all that. I'll just take the glass."

He smiled and sat down in the driver's seat next to her, holding the rejected bottle of beer. "You know, when you let go of your tough act, you can be really charming. Not that you aren't charming the other way, too. . . ." His voice dropped off while his eyes became fixed upon her in a gentle, trance-like gaze. She was helpless to do anything but return his look. Catching himself, he straightened and asked, "What kind of sandwich would you like?"

"Anything would be fine," she said, her voice revealing the sudden jittery feeling which threatened to overcome her.

He got up and slipped off his jacket, then opened a long cabinet to hang it up. Light from a full-length mirror set in the narrow door flashed into her eyes as he closed it again. Bending his long legs, he half kneeled to the floor and opened another, smaller door next to the closet. From this he withdrew sandwich meats, cheese, and a jar of mayonnaise. Reaching into the cabinet above it, he grabbed a loaf of bread and a knife. He brought all these to the small table at the back. Joey rose to follow him, hoping to be of some assistance. In a few minutes they had made two well-stacked sandwiches, and after putting the remaining food back into the icebox, took their seats at the front again.

Light pouring through the window was beginning to make Joey feel warm, so she also took off her jacket and, declining his offer to hang it up, threw it on the carpeted floor near her chair. They ate in silence for a while, enjoying the sun's warmth and keeping an eye on the trailer and van that were still as they were half an hour ago.

Soon she drew her eyes away from the situation outside and discovered Mark was staring at her. "What's wrong?" she asked.

"I was just thinking that for all your bold self-assurance, you seem to have trouble handling men."

Embarrassed, she replied, "I don't usually have any trouble."

"I think I know what the problem is. As far as I've been able to discover, your only encounters with men are in city office buildings where a certain amount of self-restraint and decorum have to be maintained. Here in the desert, men can behave more as they'd wish."

"I guess that tends to prove your theory that a woman can't take care of herself out here without a man around to protect her," she remarked with mild acidity.

"Well, it doesn't disprove it."

"I just wish men would leave me alone," she said sourly.

"Oh, come now. You don't mean that for a minute," he said with a laugh.

"Of course I do!"

"If you didn't want to attract men, you wouldn't keep your appearance so sleek and beautiful. You'd cut off all that lovely blond hair and wear dowdy clothes."

"I work in offices—I have to keep up my appearance," she countered.

"Perhaps, but you're not obligated to look like a knock-out fashion model."

"What are you trying to say?" she asked. "That I really *want* to have men chasing me?"

"I would say the evidence points to that."

"Well, I'm afraid you're wrong. I'm perfectly happy on my own. I don't need male attention to feed my ego."

"Don't you need companionship . . . love?" he asked, his voice oddly soft and low.

She looked down at her half-consumed sandwich. "That's just a lot of romantic nonsense. Men don't really care for women that way. Women would just like to think that they do. Some of us eventually wise up," she said bitterly.

"How do you know what men feel? You aren't a man,"

he said in a restrained voice, as though controlling his temper. She looked up and saw the firm challenge in his dark eyes and steady gaze.

"I know how I've been treated by men," she quietly retorted.

His eyes softened. He leaned back in the seat, silent for a moment, then said, "Tell me about your old college beau. What was he like?"

"Why do you want to know about him?" she asked rather sharply, again wondering why Mark was always so eager to dig into her past.

"Just curious. Was he a football player or something?"

She had to chuckle, remembering Robin Bloomfield's tall, but very slender physique. "No, he would have been too skinny to make the team. He wasn't much interested in sports anyway. He was studying drama."

"How did you meet him?"

"At a party. He had a bright, witty personality and nice manners. He was always the center of attention at gatherings."

"And good looking, too, I suppose."

"Yes . . ." she said quietly, her mind conjuring up the image of Robin's sandy hair and blue eyes, his light coloring and adorably handsome features. ". . . yes, he was nice looking. Kind of cute and funny."

"The type of young man you thought you could trust . . . feel safe with?"

"Yes, I suppose so," she hesitated, not sure what he was getting at.

"And with all his charm and good manners, you never suspected he wasn't being true to you."

It seemed Mark had guessed the whole story. "No, I didn't," she replied slowly. "Some . . . some of my friends warned me that he was, well . . . a flirt, but I couldn't believe it," she confessed, not knowing why she should tell Mark any of this.

"Why not?" he asked in the kindest of voices.

Her lower lip trembled slightly. "Because when he was with me, he'd always . . . stop . . . when I asked him to." She made a fluttery smile. "You see, my parents raised me rather strictly, and in those days I was always careful not to go too far with a man." Joey didn't say that things really hadn't changed at all from those days, in fact she had purposely added the phrase to make herself appear more sophisticated. She glanced up at Mark, but his dark eyes and face were impassive as he quietly listened. "Anyway," she continued in a firmer voice, "since he was always a gentleman with me, I just couldn't believe he was the kind who would try to take advantage of women."

Mark smiled, as if to himself. "It never occurred to you that he might be getting his needs met elsewhere, with easier targets?"

"No," she said with chagrin.

"Were you that much in love with him?" he asked, a touch of disbelief in his tone, as if to say, You couldn't have been.

How could she answer? She couldn't begin, nor would she want to try to convey the reverent attachment she had formed for Robin. To her he had seemed the most appealing, the most wonderful person she had ever met, and she was astounded when such an engaging and popular young man had actually shown interest in her. She had been so proud to think of him as hers during the months they had dated. "I loved him," she simply stated.

"Had you thought of marrying him?"

"I had begun to hope he would ask me when . . ." she left off, feeling it was unnecessary to complete the sentence.

51

"When . . ." he repeated, urging her to finish.

Annoyed, she quickly rejoined, "When I came back to campus early after visiting my parents and found him in my room, in the midst of seducing my roommate. It was obvious he had almost completed his mission when I unceremoniously walked in on them." Her tone was growing sarcastic. "My foolish roommate cried and cried, while Robin made laborious explanations and apologies. Fortunately, I had the wisdom not to believe any of it."

"And since then you've never trusted any man."

"I don't see why I should," she said defensively.

"You find it safer to keep men at arms' length rather than chance falling under another romantic spell."

"Who are you, Dr. Freud?" she shot at him. "What do you care what I think about men? Why do you keep asking all these questions?" she demanded.

His dark countenance, unmoved by her outburst, continued to be impassive, except for the deep intensity with which his large eyes probed hers. "Because I find you absolutely fascinating, Joey. I have to find out what makes you the way you are." He paused, and as she said nothing, he added, "There's one more question I—"

"I don't want to hear it!" she interrupted, turning her head away.

"You told me you felt safe with this fellow—that's why you liked him," he continued. "Tell me, do you feel safe with me?" His penetrating gaze remained steady and expectant.

"I . . . I don't know what you mean," she responded, very much disturbed.

"I think you do; that's why you don't want to answer," he said calmly. "You're afraid of me, aren't you? In fact, you're actually afraid of most men . . ."

Joey rose from her seat, but she felt herself being

grabbed around the waist before she could reach the door. "Let me go!" she said, wrestling against his strong arms.

"Joey, please, don't go." Mark turned her around to face him, his hands firmly clasped over her shoulders. She covered her face with both palms, hiding a fit of emotion. "It's all right," he said softly. "Don't be embarrassed about anything we've said or about what you feel. Everyone has fears." Joey didn't know what to think or feel. Meanwhile Mark's low voice continued to gently assault her sensibilities. "I just thought if we brought your feelings into the open, we could deal with them, and then perhaps you would find that you . . . could like me after all. Do you understand what I mean?"

"I don't understand anything about you," she replied, pushing out of his grasp and moving back to her seat. She sat stiffly hunched forward on the edge of the chair, her head bowed.

"I'm really not very complicated, Joey," he said, squatting in front of her. "I prefer to deal with people in a direct manner. I like you, but you don't have a very high regard for me. I just want to find out why and see if I can change your opinion."

She didn't want to look at him, but something inexorably drew her eyes to his. His voice had been calm, but his brown eyes were concerned and watchful. She had never studied him at such close range before. Her eyes moved over the smooth dark skin drawn taut over his firm jawline and high cheekbones and the straight black hair swept gently over his broad forehead. He seemed so alive and vital; she felt an unexpected desire to reach over and touch him.

The dark eyebrows drew together slightly while his eyes seemed to widen in wonder, responding to her inquisitive stare, as if he sensed that she was looking at him for the first time as a real person and had not found him unattractive.

She dropped her eyes to her lap for a moment. "I don't know why you should like me," she said shyly. "I've said some pretty nasty things to you."

He smiled with such genuine happiness, it surprised her and, curiously, made her uneasy. "That's okay," he told her. "I probably deserved it. I'll admit I sometimes deliberately provoked you just to see your reaction. But that's over with now. Now we can be more straightforward with one another, and I'm glad."

His eyes were shining with kindness and contentment, as though he had gained what he had been seeking from her. She felt strangely frightened.

He rose up, leaned forward, and peered out the front window. "Looks as though the situation outside is still the same. Would you like to play some cards?"

"Okay," she replied, glad for some distraction that would tend to hinder further conversation.

He took out a deck from one of the cabinets. "What games do you know how to play?"

"Just poker."

His shoulders shook with mild laughter. "Poker? Where did you learn that?"

"My father taught me."

"Oh, I see," he said, dealing cards onto the wooden drink holder which extended forward between the two seats. "Your father didn't have a son to teach, so he taught you instead."

Did he have to be right about everything? "I suppose so," she mumbled.

They had played several hands when their attention was drawn to the window. A sturdy truck with four-wheel drive was backing up toward the imbedded trailer. Meanwhile the van, which apparently had finally been detached

54

from the trailer, was now moving under its own power out of the water and onto dry road. Their game slowed for the next hour or so as they watched men with shovels work about the trailer while the truck was being attached to it.

At last, after much difficulty, the truck moved slowly forward, pulling the huge trailer out of the mire. Cheering and applause broke out among the throng of delayed travelers waiting about.

"Looks like we can go now!" Joey said with delight. She was surprised that Mark seemed less than enthusiastic.

"Looks that way," he echoed quietly, pulling the cards together. "You play a good game of poker, Joey."

"Thanks," she said, laughing a bit. "It's been a while since I've played. Thanks for asking me over, Mark," she added a little nervously. "For helping me out with those two men also."

"Any time." He seemed uneasy and disappointed. Not knowing what to make of him, she reached down for her jacket and stood up to go. He rose and opened the door for her, stepping down onto the ground after her.

"Good-bye," she said, extending her hand.

His eyes grew warm and sad. "You don't have to be so quick to leave," he said softly, ignoring her outstretched hand and drawing her into his arms.

She was startled. "Mark, you said there were no strings attached when you invited me in."

"No, Joey, no strings. This is for free." He pulled her close, enveloping her in a long, slow kiss. For some reason, this time it did not occur to her to resist. His mouth clung persistently to hers and she was conscious of being pressed against him while his strong hands moved slowly over her back. She was lulled by the warm, secure feeling that permeated her entire being.

At last he took his mouth from hers, then tightened his

embrace for a moment before gently releasing her. His eyes were lustrous and eager as he said, "Why don't you follow me, Joey? We're going in the same direction anyway. Why not travel together, caravan style?"

Quickly she pulled away from him. "No! No, I . . . I want to be on my own."

"But why?" he asked, clearly not understanding the wary fear he saw in her eyes.

"I don't know. I just want it that way," she said, backing away.

"Wait! Don't misunderstand," he said urgently, taking a step toward her. "I didn't mean it to be anything that . . . let's say, that your parents wouldn't approve of. I just meant that if we travel together, neither of us would be alone. It's safer that way."

"I understand, but . . . I don't want to. I'd rather be on my own, Mark. Good-bye."

She turned from him and walked quickly to her car without looking back. But imprinted in her mind were the dejected dark eyes she had sought to escape, without knowing why. All she understood was that she wanted to get out of there—away from him.

Quickly she started her car and pulled onto the road. She passed the blue van and fell into the small line of vehicles that had formed to drive slowly through the washout. After waiting anxiously for several minutes, it finally came her turn. Carefully she drove into the large pool covering the road, water spraying out from her wheels in all directions. It seemed it might become periously deep, but she continued and soon reached the other side safely, relieved that the water and Mark Chavira were behind her.

She immediately picked up her speed and moved on. Soon she was passing cars traveling at a slower pace, wanting to put as much distance as she could between herself and the blue van. She could no longer see it in her mirror, but she pressed on nevertheless, all the while a question ringing through her mind: What does he want from me? What does he want?

Chapter Four

The sun was gradually setting over the desert hills, a glowing red ball hanging amid ribbons of yellow and salmon-tinted clouds. It was growing dark and Joey was still almost eighty miles from Guerrero Negro. She had been unable to get gas all afternoon, as the service stations were invariably out of unleaded. She estimated she had little more than enough to make it to her destination and was grateful her small car made good mileage.

She had driven as fast as she dared, but constant potholes, several more small washouts, and difficulties passing slower vehicles safely on a narrow two-lane highway had slowed her progress dreadfully. Her only comfort was that she had not caught sight of the blue van since she had passed through the large washout hours ago.

Now her only goal was to make it to Guerrero Negro, which she must, as she had passed the last hotel over an hour ago, and according to her guidebook, there were none along the road to her destination. She did not mind, however, for the farther south she got, the closer she was to La Paz and the farther ahead, she hoped, of Mark

Chavira. If only she had more gas in her tank, and it wasn't growing so dark. . . .

Her thoughts returned to Mark again, to rehash what she had been turning about in her mind all afternoon. Why was he so interested in her? Why had he looked at her that way? And why should his attentions worry her so? She felt as though he were drawing her to him and would hold her prisoner if she did not stay out of his reach. She meant to keep her freedom, and somehow she was sure he wanted to ensnare her—to clip her wings and tear her apart with questions and more questions until there was nothing left to hold her together.

She listened to her own thoughts and wondered if she was becoming paranoid. What had this man done to her? She had known him only two days and already she was becoming high-strung and skittish. If she could just manage to stay away from him, she would be all right.

It was completely dark now, and she brightened her headlights to better illuminate the dim road ahead. She was coming into a hilly section and as she rounded the curves of the meandering road, her lights played upon the spindly, oddly shaped cirio trees near the highway, creating an eerie appearance. She tried to maintain her speed in spite of the fact that potholes were difficult to spot in the dim light.

After slowing to maneuver some sharp curves, she saw the road straighten ahead and purposely picked up her speed. Steadily she gained velocity until all at once the car began to vibrate violently as it sped over some unforeseen potholes and she heard the sudden sharp bang of a blowout. For several terrible seconds she could not control the car. It skidded off the road, bouncing over the rough desert floor until it came to a jolting stop amid the sound of breaking glass and grinding metal.

She sat completely stunned for a moment, barely able

to realize what had happened. It was the sudden thought that something might catch fire that propelled her to action. She opened the door, almost forgetting to unfasten her seat belt, and ran out and away from the vehicle.

For a long while she stood a safe distance away in the cold night air, studying the sight before her. One headlight was smashed, but the other still functioned, and by its light she could see that her car had run into a low, flat, outcropping rock, one edge of which jutted out of the ground high enough to do great damage to the front of her car. In addition to the headlight, the front bumper and grill appeared to be mangled, and the hood was buckled from the impact.

Much later, she slowly moved back toward the car, assuming it must be safe to do so by then. The only sound she could hear was her shoes scraping through the sandy soil, while all about her was total darkness, except for the low light of her remaining headlight starkly illuminating the desert in a ghostly manner. The sense of her aloneness in the middle of a barren landscape was beginning to make a devastating impact.

"Mark was right," she whispered fearfully into the chill air, painfully recalling all his warnings about traveling alone and driving at night. In spite of the fact that she had been trying to avoid him, at this moment she wished he were here. He would know what to do.

"You got yourself into this, you'll have to handle it alone," she said aloud, trying to conjure up her self-reliance. It occurred to her that the Green Angels would certainly be of assistance, but they only patrolled the road during the day. She would have to spend the entire night alone, and perhaps a good part of the next day also, before one came along. She shivered at the thought, realizing she hadn't eaten since noon and had no blankets. She would just have to make do with her cans of tuna and crackers and put on all the warm clothing she had brought. Yes, she could manage, she assured herself. But to be so isolated . . .

She heard a motor in the distance and soon saw a pair of headlights moving up the highway toward her. She started up with the hope of finding help, but then became wary, thinking it might be men like those she had met earlier that day who could try to take advantage of her in her predicament.

The vehicle slowed to a stop. She could just barely make out its form behind the brightly glowing headlights. She stood like a statue as she heard a door slam. Suddenly a strong beam of light reached her eyes and she was momentarily blinded.

"Joey! Are you all right?"

"Mark!" she cried, recognizing his voice immediately. She moved toward him and quickly found herself caught up in his arms.

It seemed he would squeeze the life out of her while his angry voice assailed her ears. "What the hell is the matter with you? I told you not to drive at night! Do you have to be so damned independent you won't even listen to common sense?"

"I know, Mark. You were right," she whispered against his leather jacket as she clung to his tall frame. "I just wanted to get away . . . to get to Guerrero Negro."

"Get away from me is what you meant to say. You little fool! You could have been killed!" He took a moment to control himself, then in a softer tone asked, "Were you hurt at all?"

"No, I don't think so," she replied in a broken voice, wiping away tears she could not hold back. "J-just my car . . ."

"So I noticed." Keeping an arm around her, he gently pulled her along as he strode toward the damaged automobile. He shone his strong flashlight over the smashed front end. "You really slammed into this rock, didn't you," he commented dryly as he surveyed the damage, holding the light at various angles to get the full picture. "Well, it may not be that bad after all," he added, rather to himself.

"You mean I may be able to drive it?" she asked, full of hope.

"No, I just mean I don't think you've totalled it," he replied sardonically. "I suspect your radiator's split open. You'll have to have it towed out of here. My God, what did you do to that tire?" He directed the flashlight toward the mangled rubber tube beneath the front end.

"I think I hit a deep pothole—it was hard to see in the dark—and the tire burst. I lost control and went off the road." Trying to keep herself from succumbing to emotion again, she put her hands over her face.

Mark drew Joey to him in a comforting embrace. "Don't worry, I'll take care of you," he quietly reassured her. "I don't mind."

Another emotion now beginning to take over, she tried to push away from him. "I'm okay," she sniffed.

"You've had a shock, Joey. It's better if you go ahead and cry," he told her, keeping her close.

"No, I'm all right now," she insisted in a firm voice, as she pulled out of his embrace to stand on her own.

He allowed his arms to fall back to his sides. "You don't have to prove to me you can take it like a man!" An impatient sigh escaped him. Looking toward her car, he said in a resigned manner, "We'd better turn off the lights and transfer your luggage to my van."

"You'll take me to Guerrero Negro to find a mechanic?"

"Sure—tomorrow."

"You're right, a mechanic wouldn't come out to tow it

at this time of night," she reasoned. "Well, at least we can drive in and stay at the hotel there."

Mark shook his head. "I'm not driving anymore tonight, Joey. We'll spend the night here in my van," he said in a tone that forbad contradiction.

"W-what do you mean?"

"After this you should know how dangerous it is to drive at night. I'm not going any farther until morning."

"Then why did you drive this far?" she argued, panic settling in.

"Because I didn't see your car parked anywhere along the way and I was afraid you'd try something like this. I decided I'd better keep going—against my good judgment —to make sure nothing had happened to you."

"I didn't ask you to look after me!"

"Someone ought to. You haven't done a very good job of taking care of yourself."

Humiliation increased her anger. "Why should you bother to trouble yourself about my welfare?"

He stared down at her, but his features were barely discernible in the darkness. "I don't know. It certainly isn't for the thanks I get!" He went to her car, turned off the headlight and removed her keys from the steering wheel shaft, then closed and locked the door and went around to the back.

Joey watched him quietly, her mind in too much confusion for her to be of any assistance. As always, he had evoked a myriad of feelings which left her unable to act with anything resembling purpose and reason. For the moment, regret won out over the contending emotions of anger, humiliation, and fear. "Mark, I'm sorry," she found herself saying with heartfelt sincerity. "I didn't mean to be ungrateful. I . . . I'm glad you're here."

He said nothing as he lifted her suitcase and tote bag out

of the rear compartment of her hatchback, setting them on the ground before locking the car.

"Can I help with those?" she asked in a small voice.

"Here, you can hold the flashlight." He handed it to her, and as he carried her bags to the van she walked beside him, somehow feeling like a small child who was being allowed to help Daddy.

They had reached the van and he was depositing her luggage inside when an idea occurred to her. "Mark, I could sleep in my car," she suggested. "It would give you more room in here."

He sank down onto the back seat, near which he had placed her luggage, and casually laid one arm over the small table. "I don't need any more room," he said patiently. "You'll be more comfortable and safer in here with me." Her wary expression caused him to add, "I promise you, Joey, you *will* be safe. I'm not in the mood for molesting captive women tonight."

"I didn't mean that," she hurried to say, wondering why he had chosen to use the word captive. "I'm not afraid," she asserted in a thin voice.

"No? Then you can't have any reasonable objection to sleeping in here. There won't be any tongues wagging since there's no one to see us."

Defeated by logic, Joey made no response. He got up and took a few steps to the side door, moving past her in the close quarters. She flinched as she felt his jacket brush against her breast and took a step back, bumping into the wall of the van. His hand on the door handle, he turned and looked at her. "You're not afraid of me?"

She swallowed and cast her eyes to the floor.

After sliding the door shut, he moved back to her and placed a gentle hand on her upper arm. "I would never harm you, Joey. Try to believe that." He reached down for her hand. "Come and sit in front with me. I want to find a good place to pull off the road."

She did as he asked. He drove a short distance to a pull-off and parked, then turned off the headlights and switched on the van's interior lights.

"Have you eaten anything since lunch?"

She shook her head.

"I've got some canned beef stew. How about that?"

"That would be fine, thank you," she replied, wishing her voice didn't sound like that of a well-brought-up little girl. Apparently he thought so too, for she noticed his smile as he rose from the driver's seat.

He went to a lower cabinet and withdrew what looked like a metal carrying case. He slid the door open again and took the case outside, where she watched with interest as he converted it into a tiny, two-burner stove. Following his directions, she brought out a saucepan, a tea kettle with water from the small sink, and a large can of stew.

Before long they were eating a hot meal and drinking steaming instant coffee from paper plates and cups. Afterward, she cleaned up while he repacked the portable stove.

When everything was once again in order, he closed the sliding side door and locked it. Immediately panic seized Joey's heart. She had never before been so totally alone with a man, and now she was locked in—cut off from any means of escape. She watched mutely as he took down a pillow and bedding from the upper shelf of the long closet, her heart steadily pounding in anxiety.

"I think you'll find this back seat makes a pretty comfortable bed," he told her, setting down the bedding and pulling out the small table from the hole in the floor which held its metal stem. He took the table apart and set it out of the way, then removed the seat's back pads, widening it. In a few moments he had converted it into a small, cozy-looking little bed, complete with sheets, blanket, and a pillow.

"There you are," he said, stepping back. "I guess you'll want to change into your nightgown."

"Oh, no, I can sleep in my clothes," she immediately assured him.

"Suit yourself, but I'm changing out of these," he said, indicating his own attire.

Joey's eyes widened in horror.

Mark broke into a quiet laugh, apparently unable to subdue his keen amusement over the situation. "Keep calm, Joey. I'll show you how we can manage it with the utmost propriety."

He stepped toward the driver's seat and loosened a long, heavy curtain which had been pulled together and fastened against the wall near the seat. It was held to the roof by runners, and when he pulled it across the width of the van, it completely separated the two front seats from the rest of the vehicle. "I should have enough room to change out in front and you can have the rest to yourself. How's that?"

"I guess that's okay. Wh-where will you sleep?" Her mind had already moved on to an even more formidable problem.

He smiled. "I'll put my sleeping bag down on the floor. That's how I always sleep in here. The carpeting is heavily padded and it's comfortable enough. Anything else troubling you?" The smile continued to hover at the corners of his mouth.

"No," she answered in a nettled tone, vexed that he should find it all so amusing.

"Okay. Let me get my pajamas," he said as he reached into the closet, "and then I'll leave you to yourself. Tell me when you're finished changing."

He disappeared behind the drape. Joey waited a few

cautious moments, then, keeping a watchful eye on the curtain, she opened her suitcase and pulled out her long white nightgown. She changed as quickly as she could and was careful to put all her articles of clothing back into the suitcase, then closed the lid.

Joey pulled aside the covers and slid down into the surprisingly comfortable little bed, then pulled the blanket back over her. "I'm finished now," she called out rather weakly, her hands unconsciously clinging to the blanket pulled high up under her chin.

She watched as the drape was pulled aside, then promptly stopped breathing. Mark appeared wearing only brown pajama pants, his broad muscular chest completely bare. He stopped when he saw Joey's gaping expression. "I lost the top to these long ago," he explained with a nuance of embarrassment at her stare. "In fact, I usually don't wear . . . well, never mind. I didn't mean to startle you."

While she recovered, her eyes fixed on the ceiling, he brought out and unrolled a long sleeping bag down the length of the carpeted floor. After finishing that task, he took a few steps toward her. "Are you comfortable there?" he asked, looking over the small feminine form shrinking beneath the blanket.

"I'm fine," she was quick to respond, hoping he did not intend to come any closer.

A bemused grin crossed his face. "Is there anything I can get you? A glass of water? A teddy bear?"

"No."

"I'll put out the lights, then. Good night, Joey."

" 'Night."

The lights went out and it was completely dark. Joey could hear Mark sliding into his sleeping bag and zipping himself in. After a short while, his gentle, rhythmic breathing told her he was asleep. Only then did she begin to relax and allow her mind to drift over the day's events.

Since early that morning she had used all her ingenuity and energy to try to elude Mark Chavira. Now here she was, locked in his van and lying only a few feet away from him, stranded somewhere in the middle of a desert, her wrecked car a few hundred yards away.

Strange that under the circumstances she should be experiencing the sense of secure serenity that now was stealing over her as she lay quietly in the dark stillness of the night.

Chapter Five

"It's morning, Joey." A gentle rocking motion on her shoulder accompanied the words. Pulling herself out of a sound sleep, she opened her eyes and met smiling brown ones looking down at her.

"What time is it?" she asked, sounding very groggy.

"Six thirty. We'd better get an early start. It's a ways to Guerrero Negro and we'll have to lead the mechanic back here again to tow your car."

"Yes, you're right," she said, sitting up. She noticed his brown pullover sweater and darker brown pants. "Oh, you're already dressed," she said, feeling as though she were holding up progress.

"That's okay. I'll go out and start up the stove while you change in here. How about eggs, toast, and coffee for breakfast?"

"Sounds wonderful!" She noticed he was looking at her quizzically. "What's the matter?"

"That nightgown. Did you get it out of a museum?" he asked, eyes twinkling in amusement.

She pulled the blanket up to cover herself, replying hotly, "I bought it at an expensive shop in L.A."

Breaking into a full smile, he kissed her burning cheek and ruffled her hair. In the next minute he was gone, closing the door of the van behind him.

She remained where she was for a moment, head bowed and still blushing. But a smile soon crept over her face and her eyes were warm and bright as she pushed the covers aside.

They left after breakfast and the entire morning was spent making arrangements for her car. Upon arriving in the city of Guerrero Negro, they found a mechanic with a tow truck and hours were spent driving back to the desolate spot where they had camped to pick up her car and tow it back.

Once back in the city, the mechanic explained to Mark in Spanish that the car would need several parts replaced, including the radiator, adding that it would take a week or two for some of the parts to be obtained.

"That long?" Joey gasped, when Mark had translated for her. "I'll never make it to La Paz, then," she said, deeply distressed.

"There may be some bus you could take . . ." Mark pointed out.

"Yes, I suppose so," she commented without enthusiasm.

". . . or you could ride with me. I'll be passing through La Paz on my way to Cabo San Lucas."

Her face brightened, then grew cautious. "I hate to impose on you any more than I have," she said slowly.

"It's no imposition; you won't be taking me out of my way."

Joey absently stared at the ground while pondering the situation. The thought of taking a bus to La Paz was not appealing, as she assumed she would be the only American on it and her Spanish was limited. She could stay at a hotel in Guerrero Negro and try to notify her parents to come and pick her up, but that would interfere with her father's beloved fishing schedule and would certainly spoil his vacation. Besides that, she hated to feel dependent on her parents for help. The remaining alternative—going with Mark—seemed the best.

Even so, nagging doubts lingered, making her hesitant to accept his offer. Though she had to admit that she was beginning to like him, and he had certainly been more than kind to her, there was yet something lurking beneath the surface of her emotions that made her uneasy, something that warned her to beware.

Still, she reasoned, if they left now, they would arrive in La Paz the next day, requiring them to be together only one more night. And, after all, hadn't he been quite the gentleman last night? Yes, under the circumstances, she decided, his offer was the best solution.

"All right, I'll go with you, Mark—and thanks," she told him.

"I'm glad," he replied, taking her arm to lead her to the van. "We'll leave your car here then, and you'll have to pick it up on the way back. With luck, it'll be ready and waiting for you. Before we leave, did you want to try to phone your parents? Finding a telephone may not be easy and I'm not sure how the connections would be, but we can try. They may be worried about you."

"Oh, I don't think so. I'm sure they've assumed by now that I didn't leave home until Christmas day. I'm always leaving at the last minute because of my job. They've probably heard about the roads, too, and will expect me to be delayed by the washouts. Luckily they came through ahead of the bad weather."

"Don't you think they'd be concerned?"

"I suppose my mother may be a little worried, but my

71

father's probably too busy enjoying his fishing to think much about it." She chuckled as a new thought entered her head. "Besides, if I call them, no doubt they'd ask how my car is holding up and then I'd have to tell them what happened. After that I'd have to explain how I've accepted a ride in a van with a strange man I've met on the road. I think they'd be more worried *after* the phone call!"

She was surprised that Mark seemed disturbed by her lighthearted remarks. "Yes, they probably would be," he replied in a serious tone. After taking a long breath, he shrugged his shoulders. "I guess there's nothing we can do about that now. We'd better get on our way," he said, taking her by the hand. "Let's stop at a restaurant for lunch first."

They went to a small restaurant where Joey bravely ordered the Mexican combination plate that Mark recommended. As they ate the spicy but delicious food, Mark was estimating how far they could travel that day.

"I think we can easily make it to Mulegé, barring any unforeseen problems. The roads are in better shape farther south—not so many potholes. There are several nice beaches just south of Mulegé on Bahia Concepción. They have some camping facilities, though most are fairly rustic. I usually stay there a day or two and fish. In fact, maybe we can catch supper. Do you like to fish?"

"No, not much. I'm a great disappointment to my father in that respect. I take after my mother and get seasick easily, so he goes on his fishing excursions by himself. He tried to interest me in casting from a pier, but I always thought it was kind of boring. Besides, I didn't like having to watch the poor fish flopping around, dying a slow death."

"Yes, it's a little cruel, I suppose," Mark agreed with a smile. "There's nothing like fresh fish for dinner though."

"Well, that's true," Joey had to admit.

They were silent for a while, concentrating on finishing their meal, but Mark soon broke the conversational lull. "So . . ." he said, as if thinking aloud, "seems like your father hoped you could take the place of the son he had wanted. Does he discount you now because you're 'only a woman'?"

"No, not exactly," Joey responded with a perky smile. "He always brags that I've done all right—for a girl."

Mark chuckled along with her. "I'm glad to see you can laugh about it."

"My father has his shortcomings, but I have to admit that he taught me to stand on my own two feet. He made me ambitious to form a career for myself and sent me to the best college he could afford. It was because he wanted to be proud of my accomplishments as he would a son's, and I'm grateful for that. Some fathers would raise a daughter to have lower expectations for herself."

"That's true, but it's a shame he doesn't appreciate your feminine qualities more."

The reference to her femininity made Joey self-conscious and she was glad their waiter chose that moment to bring the check. "Mark, you'll have to let me pay for this," she said, placing a finger on the slip of paper. "You've done so much for me lately."

He slowly grinned. "All right, but I assure you it's been a pleasure to come to your rescue."

In a while they were back on the road, continuing south on Highway 1, which now cut a virtually straight swath over flat, featureless desert. A few cattle could occasionally be seen amid the cactus and low shrubbery, but these were the only diversions in the landscape. The sun shone brightly through a clear sky, however, and Joey was in good spirits as she kept up a conversation with Mark.

"So, Joey, how do you feel about marriage?" The question came as a jolt after their rather academic discussion of the area's plant life.

"W-what do you mean?" she stuttered. For an instant, his words had sounded almost like a proposal.

"Well, do you want to get married eventually, or with your low opinion of men, have you vowed to remain single?"

She relaxed a bit, realizing it was just another of his probes into her psyche. "I haven't made any vow, but I imagine I'll probably stay single. I'm involved with my career, I have my own identity. It would be an intrusion to have to adjust to someone else's habits, to have to worry about pleasing a husband all the time."

"Afraid of being turned into a barefoot and pregnant housewife?"

She considered the question. "Yes, you might say that. That's what happened to my mother. She had intended to study nursing, but then she met my father and that was the end of that. She's spent the last twenty-five years cooking, cleaning, raising me, and agreeing with everything my father says. And all her years of work have gone largely unappreciated—at least by my father."

"I imagine there are many housewives who get little compensation for all the work they do, but you shouldn't assume that *all* men are like your father. How do you know you won't meet a man who doesn't mind your having a career? Someone who might encourage you and take pride in your work? Perhaps even be willing to share the housework or agreeable to the idea of hiring a cook and a maid? Are you sure such a man can't exist?"

"Do you personally know any man like that?" she queried rather smugly, giving him a steady glance.

He cautiously drummed a thumb on the steering wheel, eyes fixed on the road. "I believe I do," he said guardedly.

Something in his manner of response disturbed her.

"Well, even if such a man does exist, I'm happily independent, thank you," she asserted, turning her face toward the window again.

"I understand the value of independence, Joey, but can't you be self-fulfilled and still accept the notion that a close physical and emotional relationship with someone of the opposite sex is one of life's greatest pleasures?"

Joey shifted uneasily in her seat. "If it's so great, how come you're not married?"

He was quiet for a moment and then softly answered, "Sometimes it takes a while to meet the right person."

"But . . . you mean you would really *like* to be married?"

"Sure." His self-conscious dark eyes momentarily rested upon her before he turned them back to the road.

Joey was suddenly at a loss. What was going on here? Why were they discussing marriage of all things? The feeling of panic, which was lately becoming too familiar, crept over her. Why had he brought up the subject?

Nervously she looked out her side window trying to keep herself from fidgeting. After a moment she cautiously snuck a glance at Mark. He was silent and strangely withdrawn, eyes blankly focused on the road.

She kept quiet for a few more minutes, until the leaden silence got to be unbearable. "Do you travel in Baja California a lot?" she ventured, breaking into the strained atmosphere.

Abruptly his eyes shot to hers. "Have we changed the subject?" he asked severely. After a moment he answered in a more subdued manner, "Yes, I come down here two or three times a year."

"Why is that?" she asked as brightly as she could, hoping to hide her jarred nerves.

"I have relatives on my mother's side in Cabo San Lucas. They run a restaurant there in which I've invested, so I like to go down to visit them and see how they're coming along. They've been working on a new addition for the past year or so."

"Your expertise must be of great help to them."

"Well, they do have a lot of questions for me every time I go down there," he admitted.

"Was your mother born in Mexico?"

"Yes, but she's been an American citizen for many years. Her family came up to live in the United States for a while when she was in her teens. She married at eighteen and a short time later her parents and two younger brothers moved back. It's the two brothers, my uncles, and their sons who run the restaurant."

"Was your father from Mexico too?"

"His family was of Mexican origin, but had been in California for generations. Actually he was half Scandinavian—my grandfather married a Norwegian."

"That must be why you're so tall," she said with a grin.

"Maybe," he replied, a smile at last stealing across his uncharacteristically grim countenance.

The next several minutes passed in a more comfortable silence. Something in the distance caught Joey's eye. "Are those palm trees up ahead?"

"Date palms. We're coming to San Ignacio. It's a picturesque town—kind of an oasis in the desert—and it has an old eighteenth-century mission. Would you like to stop for a little while?"

She readily agreed and before long they were driving by a lush forest of green palms. Mark parked in the town square under a huge leafy tree with spreading branches. A magnificent old mission, built of stone, was located on one side of the square. An open market was on the other and surrounding the small park at the center were low buildings of varying design and upkeep.

Mark led Joey first toward the mission, explaining that

76

it was founded in 1728 and took fifty years to build. Before entering, they stopped to admire the huge, beautifully carved, heavy wooden doors which led inside.

The interior was small, but ornate with gold leaf and statues. Signs tacked on a wall near the entrance indicated it was still an active church.

"It's lovely," she whispered.

"Isn't it?" he agreed. "Just the right size for a small wedding," he added, looking directly at her with a playful glint in his eye.

Joey met his gaze for a moment, then turned away and headed toward the door. He followed, and when they were outside again he teased, "I detect a distinct tendency on your part to bolt at any reference to the word marriage. Would you care to explore the reasons behind your reaction with me?"

"No!" she replied, annoyed at his sudden turn for amusement.

"Afraid even to discuss it?" he prodded.

"I thought we had already discussed marriage quite thoroughly."

"But we haven't discussed why you're afraid to discuss it," he clarified.

"What? Oh, you're not even making sense anymore," she complained, not bothering to hide her irritation. They had reached his van by this time.

"We aren't ready to go just yet," he said. "I wanted to pick up a few supplies at the store over here." He pointed to a small grocery on the corner.

They spent several minutes inside buying canned goods, fresh fruit, bread, and extra bottles of purified water. They returned to the van where she quietly stood next to him, helping him put the goods into the cabinets. When they were finished, he turned her about to face him and asked

77

with an artfully winsome look in his eye, "Are you enjoying the trip, Joey?"

After a pause she replied, "Yes," unable to resist the sympathetic brown eyes that fairly begged for a positive response.

"I want you to be happy, you know. Don't let my teasing upset you."

His eyes and voice were softly hypnotic and she nodded in vague acquiescence. Slowly his lips moved down to hers and at their touch she found herself melting in his embrace. Only half aware of her reaction, she willingly returned his kiss, but soon found herself so warm and comfortable in his arms that it began to frighten her. Trembling slightly, she pushed away, but he gently pulled her back, holding her against him and tucking her head under his chin.

"Don't be afraid of it, Joey," he whispered into her hair. "Don't be afraid of your own heart."

They held fast to one another for several warm, long moments. At last he brought his hands to her shoulders, kissed the top of her head, and said quietly, "We'd better be going."

She sat down in the passenger seat while he slid behind the wheel. After starting the motor, he looked at her again, then put out a hand to caress her lightly flushed cheek. As if of one mind, they slowly leaned toward one another to enjoy another brief kiss, then reluctantly pulled apart and Mark drove off.

Joey sat quietly, her head resting against the seat's high back, not quite in touch with her own emotions but somehow blissfully content. She felt alive and happy, basking in the warmth coursing through her and not caring if it took forever to reach La Paz.

They were back on the arid desert now, winding through low hills. The van sped past a small sign.

"It's 135 kilometers to Mulegé," she quoted to Mark. "That's—let's see—84 miles," she quickly figured in her head.

Mark looked at her, eyes widened in surprise.

"Did you come to a different figure?" she asked, puzzled.

"No," he said with a laugh, "I didn't arrive at any figure. I left my pocket calculator at home." He shot her a shrewd glance and added, "I always said it was wise to keep a good accountant on hand."

As she laughed, he stretched out his hand to grasp hers, gently entwining his fingers into her slender ones. His long brown fingers felt strong and secure and she was reluctant to let go when at last he had to pull his hand away to negotiate a turn.

After a few moments of silence Mark rekindled their previous topic of conversation. "We never finished our discussion on your aversion to talking about marriage."

"Do we have to?" Joey said lackadaisically, quelling the uneasiness the subject automatically aroused within her.

"I'd like to get to the bottom of it."

"You mean after all this time you've spent psycho-analyzing me, you're still trying to figure me out?" she said, hoping to sidetrack him.

"I don't think I could ever hope to figure you out completely. You're too womanly and mysterious for a mere male to ever know what goes on inside your head."

She softly snickered. "Never mind all the soft soap. I've been flattered enough by you men to know most of what you say isn't true."

"Now that's an interesting statement to make," he said, glancing at her briefly before turning his eyes back to the road. "Why don't you believe men when they flatter you? Don't you think you're attractive?"

His questions made her pause. "Well, yes . . . I

79

. . . I know I'm attractive. Otherwise men wouldn't pay so much attention to me. But some of the things they say are just too overdone to be taken seriously. They're just trying to butter me up in hopes of getting somewhere. Take your words 'womanly and mysterious.' Now be honest. That description might apply to Greta Garbo, but not me."

"Why not? You don't think you're womanly?"

To her surprise the question made her uneasy. She didn't know how to respond. "I suppose in a way I am . . . but . . . I'm certainly no love goddess like Garbo or Marilyn Monroe."

"You don't think so? Then how do you explain all these problems you seem to have keeping men away? Only yesterday you said, after we had gotten rid of those two who were bothering you, that you wished men would leave you alone."

"How men behave is their problem, not mine," she snapped.

He chuckled softly. "I didn't mean you were to blame, but it seems to me obvious that men react to you in a positive and responsive way. Why do you think that is?"

"I don't know," she replied tersely, wishing he would get off the subject.

"Do you ever have occasion to look in a mirror, Joey?"

She sighed impatiently. "Of course."

"And what do you see in the mirror?"

She shrugged. "A girl of average height and weight with long hair."

"Only a girl?"

She drew her brows together. "What?"

"You're of age, Joey. Shouldn't you describe yourself as a woman?"

She let out another long sigh, wearying of his nitpicking. "All right. I'm a *woman* of average height with long hair."

"Average height and long hair. Is that the best you can say for yourself?"

Joey did not care to respond, for she was tired of the whole conversation.

"Would you like to know what I see when I look at you?"

"I suppose you'll tell me whether I want to know or not," she answered with sarcasm.

"I see a young woman with a slender, exquisitely shaped figure—the kind that any man could hardly pass by, beautiful hair, and a face Helen of Troy might have envied. And giving life to the image is a mysteriously complicated, unpredictable, and bewitchingly feminine personality. I mean every word of that, Joey, whether you believe it or not."

Joey's head was bowed and she was looking at her hands in her lap. It embarrassed and upset her to hear such remarks. She suspected he was exaggerating to make her feel good, yet he seemed so sincere that what he said almost took her breath away. She felt his eyes upon her now, waiting for some response. Knowing it would do no good to contradict him, she decided it would be best to try to accept the compliment graciously. "That's kind of you to say, Mark," she told him softly.

" '*Kind* of me," he repeated, shaking his head in dismay. "Tell me, Joey, did your father ever give you compliments when you were growing up?"

"Yes. Many times. He was proud of my high grades at school. And he used to brag to his friends that I was good in sports, and about the interest I took in my hobbies."

"What were your hobbies?"

"Oh, I built my own crystal set, had a model railroad . . ."

81

"Sounds like you were a tomboy!" Mark said with a smile.

"That's what my mother always said," Joey agreed, smiling now herself.

"Perhaps to please your father you unconsciously tried to be the son he wanted. You told me that one has to be a man to gain his true respect." He glanced at her to note her reaction.

She looked at him defensively. "I don't think, as a child, I would have been aware of his attitudes. Besides, I really liked the pastimes I had then."

"There's nothing wrong with a girl being interested in crystal sets and trains, but I'm wondering if *you* didn't tend to choose them because you got so much approval for pursuing them. Did your father ever tell you you were pretty?"

Joey wet her lips. "No," she replied softly, her eyes falling back to her lap.

"That's a shame, because I imagine you must have been very pretty. It seems he never validated your femininity very much. Maybe that's why you're uneasy with the idea of being attractive to men. Of course, being two-timed by your former boyfriend wouldn't have helped your self-image, either," he said with some asperity. "That guy must have been a fool." He glanced at her pensive profile. Cautiously he added, "I hope your bad experiences in the past haven't ruined your image of men forever, Joey. There may be a few of us around who are worth having, you know."

Joey caught his glance, moved in spite of herself by his earnest dark eyes. Self-consciously she turned away and looked out her side window. She could almost believe him, she thought, as she gazed out at the passing desert landscape. The beat of her heart began to quicken. If only she

82

could believe him. It might be nice . . . to be in love again. . . .

Within a few hours, after driving southeast along Highway 1, they reached the shore of the Gulf of California, the body of water which separates mainland Mexico from the Baja California peninsula. They continued south along the coast to Mulegé, passing the tropical date palms lining the river near which the sleepy town was situated. After continuing south about a dozen more miles, they reached the beautiful shores of Bahia Concepción, a large bay off the Gulf of California.

Mark pulled off the paved highway onto a steep dirt road which led several hundred yards down to and along a sandy beach, complete with picturesque thatched roof shelters constructed for campers. The clear ocean water appeared green near shore and gray-blue farther out. Across the water, small islands could be seen as well as the hilly strip of land that created the bay.

There were a number of other motor homes and tents set up along the beach. Mark pulled up next to an unused thatched shelter. Looking out the window at the bay he asked, "Do you like shrimp?"

"Yes," she replied, puzzled at the question.

"Well, then, supper may be easy tonight. See that rusty little boat anchored offshore? It's a shrimp boat. Now all I have to do is find a way to get out there. Too bad I didn't bring my rowboat this trip."

They got out of the van into the warm sea air and Joey stood by somewhat mystified as Mark took a few steps toward the water's edge and looked both ways along the beach. She watched as he walked up to the people camped next to them, apparently a family of five including three sons of varying ages.

"Shrimp boat? No kidding!" she could hear the boys'

father exclaim after Mark had spoken a few words. Within minutes the boys and their father were pulling a small rowboat into the water while Mark dashed back to the van and returned with a plastic container.

"Want to come with us?" he asked Joey as he was hurrying back toward the boat.

"Where are you going?"

"We're going to row out to the shrimp boat and buy some shrimp."

"Sure, come on along," the boys' father called to her. "We can squeeze you in."

The small boat already looked full with three boys, two of whom were almost full grown, and their father. She wondered how Mark would fit in, much less herself. "No, I get seasick," she replied, finding the best excuse she could.

Mark laughed and tweaked her nose before striding the few yards to the boat. She held her breath as the boat tipped precariously when he climbed in and took the scant space allotted him on the end seat.

Feeling rather abandoned, she watched the boat grow smaller and smaller as it gradually made its way over the gentle waves to the shrimp boat. When they reached it, she could barely make Mark out standing up in the boat to negotiate with the men on the rusting old craft. She prayed he wouldn't topple into the water.

After a few more minutes they were heading back toward shore. She breathed a sigh of relief, embarrassed at the silly tears forming in her eyes. "Joey," she whispered to herself with a rueful little smile, "I think you *are* falling in love again," admitting the feeling she had been trying hard to repress. "But it's a little scary . . ." her whispered words trailed off as she stared at the rowboat drawing nearer the shore.

"Hey, Mom, we got some shrimp!" the youngest boy

shouted as they were maneuvering the boat onto the beach.

Mark called his thanks to the owners of the rowboat as he strode toward Joey. "Dinner, madame," he intoned, as he presented her with the container full of shrimp.

"They look good," she said brightly, trying not to notice the smell as she took the container. "Did you have to stand up in the boat like that?" she complained, her voice growing small and high-pitched.

He smiled broadly. "I saw your worried little face as we started rowing out," he said, tweaking her nose again. "I can swim, you know. Anyway, I had to pay the men for the shrimp. Standing up was the only way."

"Oh . . ."

He put an arm around her waist and pulled her to his side. "You know, Joey, I think you're beginning to like me. Hmmm?"

"Yeah . . ." she sheepishly admitted, softly drawing out the word.

"Yeah," he imitated before kissing her on the nose. "Let's get supper going," he said, moving her along at a faster pace toward the van. "Do you cook shrimp in any particular way?"

She regarded him with some alarm. "I don't know anything about cooking shrimp!"

His free hand rose to his hip. "Look, lady, I just put the groceries on the table. Cooking is woman's work," he deadpanned.

"Huh?"

He laughed as he drew her nearer. "I'll give you a cooking lesson, Joey."

A short time later he had her mincing garlic on a paper plate while he set up the portable stove. "Do you cook much for yourself?" he asked as she was sitting on the step in the van's doorway, a large travel book on Mexico across her lap to support the thin plate.

"Just breakfast. I eat lunch out."

"What about dinner?"

"Well . . ." She hesitated to tell the truth. "I eat with my parents every night. My apartment isn't far from their house."

"No wonder you don't know how to cook! Sounds to me like you've been spoiled," he declared.

"It saves me time," she pointed out in her own defense, "and my mother feels better knowing that I'm eating well. You know how mothers are."

"Spoiled brat!" he said with mock piety. "By the way, what does your father do for a living—when he's not fishing."

She smiled. "He's a real estate broker, but he's been easing into retirement the last few years."

"Really? What's his name?"

"Ed Scott."

Mark shook his head. "I guess I haven't run across that name. But, then, my dealings are all in Orange County. He works in the L.A. area, I suppose."

"Yes, he does," she told him. Then with a sigh she asked, "I've finished the garlic. Anything else I can do?"

"Do you know how to cook rice?"

"Maybe. Are there directions on the box?"

"You're in luck," Mark said, laughing. "You'll find it in the upper cabinet."

Smiling, Joey rose and stepped up into the van. There were two upper cabinets, so she tried the one to the left first. As she pulled the door open, a paper accidentally fell out, landing near her foot. Looking into the cabinet, she surmised quickly that she had chosen the wrong one. It was filled with odds and ends: an old pair of sneakers, a broken pair of sunglasses, a number of guidebooks, and other papers. She began to close the cabinet door, but then remembered the paper that had fallen. Bending to pick it up, she saw it was an envelope, its contents knocked halfway out.

The letter inside appeared to be written in Spanish. As she took it in her hand and stood up again, casually noting the return address on the envelope, a photograph slipped out and fell to the floor. She bent down again to retrieve it, and then wished she had never seen it.

It was a photograph of a very young woman, exceptionally pretty, with long, shining black hair, sparkling dark eyes, and a smile that was carefree and beguiling. She was pictured from the waist up wearing a sundress, and what was revealed of her slender figure and well-formed bosom was equally devastating. A sharp pang of jealousy ran through Joey as she quickly reinserted the photograph into the envelope and threw it into the cabinet, closing the door.

Well, I couldn't expect to be the first woman he's ever taken an interest in, she silently chided herself as she opened the next cabinet. She spotted the package of rice and took it out. Still, she thought, the woman in the picture seemed rather young for Mark; she appeared to be barely more than a girl, eighteen at most. Joey would have thought that Mark would be attracted to someone a little more sophisticated.

Her jealousy becoming mixed with resentment now, Joey wondered if Mark was still seeing the girl. She remembered the return address written on the envelope—Cabo San Lucas—and wondered how he managed to keep a romance going when he only visited the city two or three times a year. Of course he hadn't mentioned how long he stayed on each visit, Joey thought waspishly.

But perhaps the romance, if indeed there was one, was

over. Would he be showing such interest in her if there were already someone else in his life?

Joey tried to concentrate on the directions for the rice, when another thought came to her. Didn't he say he had relatives in Cabo San Lucas? Maybe this girl was a relative. Of course! That would explain everything very easily. That must be it! Mark wasn't one to go about robbing cradles, however attractive the babe might be. It was probably just a photograph of a cousin or niece sent to him by one of his relatives, probably the girl's doting parents.

Happier now, Joey reread the directions on the box she was holding. But her questioning mind pulled her thoughts away again. Somehow it seemed illogical that a handsome bachelor would keep with him a picture of a girl so beautiful if she were only a relative.

"Oh, you're just being silly!" Joey admonished herself aloud.

"Are you having some problem with the rice?" Mark called from outside. "I hear you muttering to yourself."

"No, Mark. I . . . I think I've got it figured out," she called back, glad he couldn't see her embarrassed face.

About forty-five minutes later they were sitting on the sand under the thatched shelter enjoying rice smothered with shrimp in a beer-and-garlic sauce, and canned mixed vegetables. The sun was setting and it was growing dark and chilly. Joey buttoned up her jacket and sipped her hot coffee. "This meal was wonderful, Mark. How come you know how to cook? Most men don't take much interest in it."

"I see I have to remind you that the greatest chefs in the world are men. I've just learned a few easy ways to prepare seafood, since I camp and fish every once in a while. It's my mother who's the real expert. She can make anything taste good."

"My mother's a good cook too. I haven't been able to develop her proficiency at it."

"I know what it is: You're afraid of getting stuck behind a stove," he said with a knowing look.

"As a man, you don't have to worry about such things," she pointed out.

"I'll give you that, but let's not get into the battle of the sexes again."

"Afraid you'll lose?" she impishly countered.

"No . . ." he said, putting down his cup and empty paper plate. In an instant he was upon her, playfully wrestling her to the ground. As he pinned her down he said, looming over her, "You made some comment about losing?"

"Might doesn't make right!" she declared through her giggles.

Slowly and deliberately he lowered his face until their noses were the merest centimeter apart. "If you have might, you don't need to be right, little girl." His mouth came down on hers, pressing her head into the sand as the full weight of his chest relaxed over hers, snugly imprisoning her body beneath him. Her arms came up over his shoulders, pulling him closer as she revelled in the warmth and feel of his strong, manly body.

Her soft, full mouth eagerly responded to the insistent pressure of his lips, but as their passion grew, he suddenly stopped the kiss and came back up to a sitting position, drawing her up with him. When he had caught his breath a little, he said, as he cradled her in his arms, "I don't know if I can handle the new you, Joey. You go to my head."

She gave a little laugh and snuggled closer. "Hey, wait a minute," he said, edging away. "How about some more coffee?" He rose and picked up the pot, then poured them both some more. After turning on the light inside the van, he settled himself next to her again, but at a little distance.

The light through the van's open door shone softly over the sand in front of them and gently illuminated their faces. It was quite dark now, and stars were beginning to appear in the night sky. Gentle waves lapped softly on the shore a few feet away.

"I can see why you like to camp here," Joey said as she enjoyed the atmosphere and her proximity to the handsome man beside her.

"Baja California has a lot of nice places, but with the new road a lot of them are becoming overrun with tourists. I'm beginning to wish I had kept the beat-up old Jeep I used to have. The four-wheel drive enabled me to go out into the back country on primitive roads regular cars can't handle. Out there you're really alone with nature—of course you have to do without modern comforts, but it's worth it."

"Why didn't you keep the Jeep, then?"

"I decided to buy the van and didn't want to have both vehicles besides my two cars. My house is big, but I don't have that much garage space."

"But I still don't see why you bought a van when you liked the Jeep so much," she said, puzzled.

He forced a sigh. "Well, that's what happens when a man starts traveling with a woman. They're not much for roughing it, you know." He glanced at her, as though waiting for her to rise to the bait. Her face remained expressionless, however, as though she hadn't heard. After a moment he gave a light shrug and took a sip from his cup.

But Joey *had* heard: ". . . traveling with a woman." The words reverberated in her mind. The image of the beautiful girl in the picture flashed before her. She sat stunned, then grew cold inside as another vivid memory overtook her: the conversation she had overheard in the restaurant between Mark and Ted Morley. Had her growing love made that odious insight into Mark's private life slip from her mind?

Mentally groping, she recalled that Ted had asked him if he was going to Cabo San Lucas to pick up a woman; yes, she could remember the whole conversation. "That's right," were Mark's exact words in answer to the other man's casual query. And then it had become clear that Mark was single. In fact, Ted had joked that with this "lively little thing" to "take care" of Mark, he could understand why Mark hadn't "bothered" to get married.

Joey's mind went further back to the first time she saw him at the gas station in Ensenada—leering at a redhead. Joey shuddered, recalling the sensually intimate way he had then looked at her, a woman he had never even met. How could she have allowed herself to be taken in? The way he had dogged her steps, made advances, forced his company on her—it must all be a part of his technique. She was attractive enough to suit him and he was in the mood for another conquest—at loose ends with his old standby away in Cabo San Lucas. What a stroke of luck for him when her car broke down! Now he could play the gallant rescuer, take his time . . . and he probably expected her to be more than just grateful.

"Joey! You're spilling your coffee," Mark said as he took the cup from her hand. "What's the matter? Are you all right?"

"Yes," she whispered.

"Are you sure?" he asked insistently, brushing back the hair which had fallen forward over her face.

She leaned out of his reach. "I'm fine—just tired, that's all."

"It's been a long day," he sympathized. "Maybe you'd like to go to bed?"

She turned on him sharply with large, wary eyes.

"Joey, what's the matter with you?" His voice was full of concern as he moved closer and attempted to put an arm about her.

"Don't touch me!" she warned, scrambling out of his grasp.

"What?"

"I think I know what you're up to, Mark, and I'm not going to play into your hands anymore."

He studied her a moment. "I don't know what on earth you're talking about."

"No?" she taunted. "I had you pegged right the first time I saw you—just another woman chaser on the make. I don't know how I could have been so foolish! But then you do have an unusual strategy."

Mark's expression grew taut. "Would you mind stating clearly what you're getting at."

"Certainly! I'm just here to help you pass the time until you get back to your girl friend in Cabo San Lucas, isn't that right?" The question was more an accusation.

"What girl friend?"

"Oh, come now. I suppose you don't recall telling me a few minutes ago that you bought your van because you started traveling with a woman."

He suddenly began to laugh. "You misunderstood what I . . ."

"Did I?" she sharply interrupted. "Perhaps you didn't know I overheard your conversation with Ted at San Quintin. He asked if you were going down to pick up your woman, and you told him you were. I assume that's the woman you travel with—unless, of course, there are others."

He was staring at her grimly. "You sure have a creative mind."

"My mind didn't invent that conversation!" she said,

glaring back. "And then there were all of Ted's tactless innuendos. He obviously knew you were going after me. Apparently he's familiar with your habits!"

He took a long breath and dropped his eyes to the ground. "Ted has a creative mind, too." He lifted his eyes back to her face. Staring levelly into her eyes, he said quietly, "Joey, I have no other woman."

"Do you expect me to believe that? After words I've heard from your own mouth?" She would have told him of the picture she had seen, but did not want it to appear that she had been snooping in his personal belongings.

"It's possible there could be a perfectly innocent explanation . . ."

"I'm sure! If anyone could come up with one, you certainly could!"

He took a handful of sand and threw it to the side. His dark eyes pierced through the night air in fiery glimmers. "I thought that you and I had established a trust in one another. I thought that we were . . . close friends, at least. But a friend wouldn't jump to conclusions on the basis of a casual statement, or on an overheard and partially understood conversation. A friend would be patient and trusting—"

"Oh, don't start psyching me out again!" she interrupted. "I must say you do have an ingenious technique— attacking a woman's vulnerabilities until you've got her so confused she thinks she's falling in love with you. I must have caught on to your scheme just as you were going to move in for the kill!"

As if this were too much, he suddenly rose to his feet and walked toward the van. He stopped by the open door and turned around. His penetrating eyes studied her softly lit face for a moment before he strode back, coming down on one knee directly in front of where she was sitting. Placing both hands on the sand for balance, he leaned forward until his face was only inches from hers. In a husky voice, he said, "A few minutes ago we were kissing. I could have easily let it escalate into more than that, but I didn't. If I were trying to seduce you, don't you think I would have done it then?"

She leaned away from his intimidating stare, but her voice remained adamant. "That's no doubt just part of your method for developing trust. You probably con a woman into believing that making love with you is *her* idea!"

He pushed himself up again and stood before her, looking down at her implacable, upturned face. "You're so afraid of a close relationship, you'll jump at straws and cling to them just to save yourself from one! You're still frightened of me and you'd do anything to sabotage your feelings about me because they scare you, too. Opening up to another person—trusting a man—is just too frightening, isn't it? You're so much safer in your own little neuter world!"

She stood up and brusquely walked past him. "You can continue with this monologue if it'll help you save face. I'm going to sleep."

He caught her arm and turned her around again. "Aren't you afraid I'll try to take advantage of you?" he taunted, a dark light flickering through his eyes.

"Under the circumstances, I think it would be best if you took your sleeping bag and slept outside tonight," she told him disdainfully.

She began to move away, but he pulled her back, keeping a tight grip on her arm. "I think you've forgotten what the circumstances are. *You're* traveling with *me*. I won't be turned out of my own van!"

She stood perfectly still, her pulse quickening, while the grip on her arm tightened even more. "*I'll* sleep outside then."

"No, you won't. It's too cold at night for greenhorns like you. Besides,"—his voice grew sly and harsh—"what makes you think you'd be any safer out here?"

She swallowed as the blood drained from her face and her gray eyes grew large. "You said last night you would never harm me," she said in a small voice.

"But you've decided not to believe anything I say. Why should I care what I do?" His voice was quiet and his eyes piercing.

Her breathing grew shallow. Suddenly she felt very helpless.

"Go inside and change," he ordered in a low voice while he released his vicelike grip on her arm.

Her eyes widened in fear. "Mark . . ." she whispered through trembling lips.

"Well, go on!" he said in a stronger tone, giving her a small shove toward the van. She obeyed and went inside. He slid the door closed behind her.

With shaking hands she took off her clothes and put on her long white nightgown, then slipped her navy robe over it. Hands clenched, she sat down on the back couch to try and think what to do. Would he really try to . . . ?

Abruptly the door slid open and Mark stepped up into the van, shutting the door behind him, locking them in. He looked in her direction. "All ready, I see," he muttered. He walked over and lifted out the small removable table, placing it against the wall. With a tired sigh he said, "Here, I'll make up your bed." After he had taken down the linens from the closet, he looked at her again. "Well, you'll have to get up," he told her in a short tone of voice.

She quickly rose and moved out of the way to stand with weakening knees near the door. In a few more minutes, her little bed was all prepared. He turned toward her and she took a step backward, her gray eyes frozen in fear.

"For heaven's sake, Joey, I'm not going to touch you!"

95

he said with impatient anger. "Get under the covers and go to sleep. Maybe it'll help clear out some of the tangled weeds in your brain!"

Chapter Six

"Rise and shine, Joey." The words cut through the webs of sleep to the accompaniment of splashing water. "Come on, it's eight o'clock. I've let you sleep as long as I could."

Clumsily Joey rolled over and opened her swollen, red-rimmed eyes. She saw Mark standing at the small sink, wiping his face with a towel. She guessed he had been shaving. He was dressed in a light shirt and pants and his hair was wet.

"Maybe I should give you a dunk in the ocean," he said, throwing her a glance. "The water's nice and cold—it'd wake you up in a hurry."

"Is that what you did?" she asked in a scratchy voice. "Your hair is wet."

"Since there aren't any shower facilities here, it was a viable alternative. I'll let you change in here while I start breakfast," he said, moving toward the door. He closed it behind him and she was alone.

She heaved a deep sigh and rubbed her eyes. Life seemed so miserable. Even the sky was overcast and the ocean looked leaden, she noted, as she pushed aside the thin window curtain over her bed. She wished she could have slept better. It was only a few hours ago that she finally had drifted into a deep sleep. Maybe a dip in the ocean was a good idea; she felt grubby since there had been no chance to bathe the day before.

With another sigh she threw aside the covers and got up. In a few minutes she had found and changed into her green bikini, tied her hair atop her head, and was looking in her tote bag for the extra towel she had brought.

When Joey appeared outside, the towel draped over her shoulders, Mark did a double take. "You're really going in?" he said, much surprised. "Don't stay too long—you'll get pneumonia!" he told her sternly.

Joey walked the few feet to the water's edge, shivering a bit in the sharp breeze. The weather had done a turnaround from the soft sunny day they had enjoyed yesterday. She dropped her towel to the sand, inhaled deeply, and took a running plunge.

The temperature of the water was a sudden shock, making Joey gasp, while the sharp edges of seashells hurt her feet. Calling up all her stamina, she managed to endure a few minutes in the frigid water until she heard Mark admonish her to come back.

She moved toward shore where he was waiting, holding her towel. Quickly he put it around her shivering body and walked with her to the van. He reached in and grabbed his own towel and helped to dry her gooseflesh.

"N-not s-so rough," she complained.

"We have to get back the circulation," he said, rubbing her slender arms. "Look, your fingernails are blue. At least you didn't get your hair wet."

He reached to wipe away a stray drop trickling down her neck, while his eyes scanned her face. "You didn't sleep well last night, did you?" he asked softly. "Neither did I. You kept me awake with your sniffling and stifled sobs." His eyes peered into hers. "Were you crying because you were still frightened, or because you were sad about the rift between us?"

She bowed her head and he draped his towel over her shoulders. Casually he brought his hands down to her bare waist and firmly pressed them against her soft flesh. The intense warmth of his hands sent new shivers through her.

"Joey," his voice caressed her ears, "let's stop all this nonsense. You know there's something between us— something wonderful. Don't let it die."

He raised one hand to her chin and tilted her face upward. His mouth felt warm on her cold lips; she clung for an instant, then turned her head to one side. "No. Stop it!"

"You liked it yesterday," he murmured, pressing his lips against her delicate throat.

"Before I was reminded what a womanizer you are!" she cried, pushing both hands against his chest to get out of his clutches. "There's nothing between us. There couldn't be!"

"You know that's not true!" he said, grasping her roughly by the shoulders. "You care for me as much as I care for you!"

"You only care about one thing!" she said through clenched teeth. "I don't want you or any other man! You're all the same underneath!" She brushed past him and locked herself in the van.

A while later she reappeared, fully dressed, in blue slacks and a white T-shirt under her jacket. Mark had been preparing breakfast. He silently handed her a paper plate of eggs and toast and poured her a cup of hot coffee.

An atmosphere of offended gloom prevailed over their breakfast, accompanied only by the sound of the increasingly large waves washing up on shore and the distant laughter of other campers' children at play. The sky grew more overcast, blocking out the sun, with rain threatening.

"What time do you suppose we'll arrive in La Paz this afternoon?" Joey asked coolly, breaking a long silence.

"What makes you think we'll get to La Paz today?" he responded with equal frigidity.

"It's only about three hundred miles. We should be able to make that," she said with alarm.

"Not if we stop at Loreto to fish."

"Why should we do that?" she asked, incredulous.

"Because that's what I always do when I pass this way."

"But . . ."

"Must I remind you again that you are along only out of the kindness of my heart? *I'm* in no hurry to get to La Paz, and if I choose to spend the day fishing, that's my privilege."

"But, Mark, my parents are waiting."

"You didn't have much concern for them yesterday," he reminded her.

"Because I thought I'd be with them today!"

"That's just too bad, Joey," he said, beginning to pack up the portable stove. "If you had listened to my advice in the first place and not driven at night, you wouldn't be in this fix."

"You're doing this on purpose, aren't you? Out of spite!"

"An insensitive male like me? Why would I bother?" he said lightly. "Maybe I just enjoy fishing—like your dad."

Deeply incensed, she threw her half-filled cup of coffee at him, but the strong wind caused it to miss its target. "I hate you, Mark!" she raged. "Of all the rotten men I've had the misfortune to meet, you are the worst!"

His eyes flared in anger and for a moment he seemed ready to lunge at her. She stopped breathing and unconsciously braced herself. But in another instant, his temper

100

was under control. He went back to his work on the stove and muttered unsympathetically, "You have your troubles, don't you, Joey?" She turned away to hide her frustrated tears.

After two long, silent hours on the road, they reached the town of Loreto on the Gulf of California and Mark parked the van at the beach near where a long pier extended into the water. The rain that had threatened never came and the clouds had now broken up, allowing bright sunshine to prevail. But the air was still crisp and strong winds caused frothy waves to wash up on shore.

Mark pulled out his fishing gear, then made himself a sandwich. After taking a bottle of beer from the ice box, he turned to Joey. "I'll be out on the pier. You can join me if you like—I have another rod."

"No, thanks!"

"Okay, stay here and mope then. Don't forget to eat lunch," he called in an offhanded tone as he stepped out of the van.

Her chin quivering, Joey watched through the window as his long, easy strides took him across the beach and down to the end of the pier. *How could he be so rude and unfeeling! This trip would have turned out fine if only I hadn't run into him!*

Restlessly Joey got up and paced the short length of the van. How to pass the afternoon? She could eat, but she wasn't hungry. It was too cold to sunbathe.

"I know," she said to herself as she reached to the floor for her shoulderbag. "I've been meaning to do this anyway." She took out a pencil and a piece of paper from a note pad she always carried. Sitting down at the small table in the back, she began to estimate and then list her share of all the expenses they had accrued since traveling together.

She guessed at the monetary value of the food she had

eaten from his ice box and the shrimp from the night before. Her accountant's mind had carefully noted and mentally stored the exact amounts he had paid each time they had stopped for gasoline, which fortunately had been in plentiful supply since Guerrero Negro. She listed half of each gas payment along with the food expenses.

After some time the listing was complete up to and including that morning's breakfast. She would add on all further expenses until they reached La Paz, where she intended to repay him down to the last centavo. Receiving only money in return for his assistance might be a disappointment for him, but it would put her conscience at ease regarding any debts she owed him, she reasoned.

That task accomplished, she was again at a loss for something to do. She bristled at the thought that this was the way her mother usually spent the larger part of her vacations—sitting around waiting for her father to come back from fishing. She was certainly not going to follow that example! There was no reason at all why she needed to stay in the van. Why not walk the short distance to town and do some exploring on her own?

She grabbed her bag and jacket and did just that. It was a small town with low buildings of various sizes and ages strung closely together along its narrow streets. The most impressive feature was a graceful stone mission with a bell tower that dominated the town.

She found herself among other American visitors as she walked down the sidewalk toward the mission. A family with lively, joking youngsters entered with her and she was amused by their banter.

Next to the mission was a small museum. She paid the admission fee of a few pesos and walked about studying the collection of displays and artifacts. It was warm inside and she was unzipping her jacket when two young men came in. They were rather clean cut types, one blond and the other a redhead with freckles. They nodded and gave her a brief hello, obviously having ascertained that she was a fellow American.

As they walked about for a while, Joey noted that the redheaded young man frequently tried to catch her eye with a kind of shy smile. "Have you been in this town long?" he asked at last.

"No, I just got here today," she replied, returning his smile.

"Oh, I thought maybe you were staying here with your family or something. By the way, my name is Ray and this is Keith."

"I'm Joey. Nice to meet you. Are you from California?"

"Yeah, Los Angeles. We're students at U.C.L.A. We came down here on the winter break."

"I'm from L.A. too. What are you studying at the university?" she asked with interest.

"Business administration," they droned in unison.

She chuckled at their unenthusiastic response. "I know how you feel. I majored in accounting and it does get pretty tiresome cracking the books day after day."

"Are you traveling down here on your own?" Ray asked, puzzled.

"No . . . well . . . yes, actually I am on my own," Joey began, flustered at the question. "I started out alone, but then my car broke down. A man I happened to meet offered me a ride to La Paz, where I'm to join my parents. I was hoping to get there today, but he decided he wanted to do some fishing here," she summarized, not quite able to keep the bitterness out of her voice.

They were finished with the museum in a short time and were walking back out onto the street. Ray, the redhead, whispered something to his friend. Keith nodded and said to Joey, "We're leaving now for La Paz. You can ride with us if you like."

The offer took her by surprise. "Oh, no, I couldn't . . ."

"We have plenty of room," Ray said. "You could be with your parents this evening. Besides, don't you feel kind of uneasy about staying alone overnight with this guy you just met on the road? Did you know him before?"

"No," Joey said, coloring a bit. "I don't know you, either," she pointed out good-naturedly.

"You've got a point there," Ray said with a chuckle. "But like I said, La Paz is only a few hours away and you could be there tonight if you come with us. It's up to you."

What a dilemma, thought Joey. On one hand nothing would make her happier than to be safe and sound with her parents. The image of Mark coming back from his fishing to an empty van was also tempting. On the other hand, she didn't know these two any better than she knew him, though they seemed sincere and respectable enough.

"Joey, what are you doing here?" a familiar, quiet voice from behind interrupted her thoughts.

She started at the sound. "Just . . . just looking around the town," she said, glancing quickly at Ray and Keith.

Mark moved to her side and put an arm about her waist. "How about coming back to the beach now?" he asked in a pleasant enough tone, but she could detect an underlying hint of implacability.

Joey's heart was pounding, as though she were an escaped prisoner, caught by her jailer, seeing her one chance at freedom fading quickly. She felt the arm of steel pulling at her waist. "Okay," she whispered, bowing her head.

"Are you going to be all right?" Ray asked, putting out a hand to detain her.

"She'll be perfectly all right," Mark assured them and continued escorting her away from the mission in the direction of the beach.

When they were about a block away, he said, "Would you have gone with them?"

Joey's heart sank as she realized he had overheard their plotting. Recovering, she said with rancor, "Why not? They could have taken me to La Paz tonight."

For a moment his eyes took on a stricken look, then reverted to a masklike appearance. "How can you be sure that's all they would have done?"

"They seemed very nice!" she retorted. "They were concerned about me."

"Just good Samaritans? You don't think your long blond curls and form-fitting T-shirt had anything to do with it?" he said, looking her over.

Startled, she looked down at her open jacket and quickly rezipped it. "Not all men are like *you*. I didn't notice *them* ogling me."

"You're being inconsistent, you know. This morning you claimed men were all alike. Just because they didn't openly stare at your shapely bosom doesn't mean they didn't notice."

"Do you have to be so crude?" she said with disgust.

"You're the one who chose your attire this morning. Are you going to blame a man for looking? I suppose I wasn't supposed to have noticed your skimpy bikini, either. Why dress like a woman if you don't want to be one?"

"What is that supposed to mean?"

"For a girl who claims she doesn't want or need masculine attention, your manner of dress today seems heavily geared to attract it. Maybe you'd better spend some time trying to figure out what it is you really *do* want," he said as they reached the van.

Joey's voice was hushed with anger. "I suppose in your conceited way of looking at things, you think that what I want is you!"

He stared at her steadily. "You said it, Joey, not me."

"My heavens, you're intolerable!" she choked out. "You are the most vain, loathsome creature that . . ."

"Save it. We've been over that ground before," he told her impatiently. "I'll be out on the pier." He turned to go, then stopped and faced her again, a severe, parental look in his eye. "Stay here by the beach, will you? I don't want you going back into town."

"So you can keep an eye on me?" she said with spiteful sarcasm.

"You have a propensity for getting into trouble."

"And you've elected yourself my warden. What if I get bored?" she taunted.

"Then come and tell me, and I'll go for a walk with you. Otherwise, stay here. I don't want my girl" —astonished gray eyes checked his words— "I don't want you walking around by yourself, collecting followers eager to help an enticing damsel in distress!" On that angry note, he turned and walked in the direction of the pier.

His girl! By what right did he call her that? Joey steamed. Talk about collectors! Wasn't he the one who, by all indications, had a harem of women scattered about, waiting on him? Well, one anyway, in Cabo San Lucas; and he obviously was trying to add herself to his menagerie. His girl! She stormed into the van and slid the door shut with a strong shove.

It was warm inside and she restlessly shrugged off her jacket, revealing her much maligned T-shirt. "I didn't know it had shrunk," she muttered to herself. "Why should I wear my good clothes just to sit around in a van all day!" she peeved.

Her eyes came across the ice box and she was reminded that she hadn't yet eaten lunch. With a sigh she opened the small compartment, took out some sandwich meats and bread, and the last cold bottle of beer. She found some unrefrigerated bottles stored in a corner and put two in the ice box before reclosing it.

After making her sandwich, she found the bottle opener and, placing the bottle on the waist-high sink top, set about uncapping it. She always had a hard time with bottles—the caps seemed tough and the openers were never shaped to grab hold easily. This one proved no exception. After a few false starts, the opener finally latched onto the cap, but in giving it her most powerful—and frustrated—grip, she managed to tip the bottle over just as the cap was coming off. In an instant her T-shirt was soaked in cold, foamy beer.

"Oh, great!" she fumed, setting the half full bottle upright and grabbing her towel, which was drying over the back of the driver's seat. She mopped up herself, the sink, and what had spilled on the carpet.

"I guess I'll have to change this top," she mumbled, uncomfortable with the sticky feel of the wet material and the smell of the beer. She noted ruefully that the wetness had made the T-shirt transparent and the outlines of her bra could be clearly discerned. "God forbid he should see me like this!"

She drew the curtain behind the driver's seat to prevent anyone from seeing through the front windows and made sure the van's back window curtains were in place. Thus secured, she took off her T-shirt and bra. After a quick washup at the sink, she knelt down by her suitcase on the floor and pulled out a long-sleeved yellow print blouse which buttoned down the front. Putting it aside for the moment, she searched through the pockets of her suitcase for a clean brassiere.

The sound of footsteps coming near the van made her stop suddenly. She paused a second to make sure her ears hadn't deceived her. The footsteps on the pavement were very close now. In a panic she grabbed her blouse and had just gotten her arms through the sleeves when the sliding door suddenly began to move. She was pulling the front sides of the garment together to cover her when Mark stepped up into the van.

"My line broke . . ." he began, then stopped as his eyes took in her state of semi-undress.

"I s-spilled beer on my T-shirt," she said, trying to steady her voice as she clutched more tightly to the front opening of the blouse. "Would you wait outside until I'm finished changing, please?"

His eyes honed in on her in a dark, set stare, an odd light giving them increased lustre. He shook his head just slightly, but his eyes did not move as he said, "That glimpse of you was too tantalizing." He took a step back, slid the door shut, and moved toward her. His voice was smooth and low as he knelt in front of where she was sitting huddled on the floor. "You looked so sweet and soft just now, Joey, like the warm, responsive woman I know you can be. Let's see if we can find the real you."

Her heart almost stopping with panic, she said in a small voice as she tried to edge backwards, "Leave me alone, Mark."

"That isn't what you want, is it?" he said, shrugging off his leather jacket and tossing it aside.

Her eyes widening as she watched him, she strove to regain her wits. Assuming a brazen look of outrage to hide her deep fright, she taunted, "You think any woman will eagerly melt in your arms, don't you? Well, you're wasting your time with me. This is one woman who's immune . . ."

"Are you?" He leaned forward and pulled her into his arms.

"Leave me alone!" she cried, trying to squirm out of his grasp and deeply conscious of the warm lips pressing against her neck, making her skin quiver.

"Never," he breathed. "You'll be mine, whatever it takes." She sensed his passion was growing out of control as he covered her face and throat with hard, tender kisses and his arms held her captive. She was helpless to do anything against such masculine strength and felt herself succumbing to his unyielding persistence.

A small moan escaped her lips when his warm, somewhat rough hand slipped beneath her unbuttoned blouse to firmly caress the softness beneath. His mouth came down on hers and she was lost in sensual oblivion, unconsciously pulling him closer with her arms, answering with her lips, and wanting nothing but him.

"I knew it could be like this between us," he whispered against her cheek some long moments later. He held her away from him a bit and gently stroked her hair, his hand coming to rest over her ear. "You're so beautiful," he murmured, his eyes a soft, yearning brown. "Look at you now—no trace of fear, just warm and eager and loving."

Carefully holding her against him, he leaned forward and pulled open the long closet door just behind her. The full length mirror shone its reflected soft light as the narrow door swung aside. He lifted her up slightly and carefully turned her about until she was facing her own image in the lower part of the long, silvery glass.

"Look at yourself," he gently urged, his hands clasped about her rib cage, as he peered at her reflection from over her shoulder. "See how womanly you are now, your hair falling over your breasts, your mouth soft and yielding, and your eyes—look at your eyes—so tender and longing." He gave her a little shake. "Do you see yourself?"

Lost in the mesmerizing flow of his low voice and his physical nearness, she strained to bring herself together, to focus her shining, softened eyes on her own reflection. How curious she looked, she thought as she regarded herself—like a little waif with her hair tossled about, her eyes needy and vulnerable, and her mouth pink and rounded from his kisses.

"Do you still deny that you need a man's love, Joey? Can you still say that you don't want me?"

She saw his intent eyes upon her in the mirror and gave herself a mental shake. She looked again at her own reflection, this time in conscious reality, and she became appalled. Like some woman of loose morals, her bosom was half uncovered, her hair unkempt, and her expression wanton. She stiffened and pulled her blouse together, bowing her head to hide her face in shame.

"Joey, what's wrong?" Mark asked, his voice troubled.

She turned on him, her eyes full of the recognition that he had nearly achieved the ultimate this time in stripping her defenses and using her vulnerabilities. "I despise you," she said in a hissed whisper full of fury and hate.

He seemed stunned with disbelief, then his eyes narrowed in intense rage. With a swift, infuriated movement, he snatched up his jacket and in an instant was gone, shoving the door closed behind him with such force that the van shook with his vengeance.

In a moment all was quiet as his footsteps faded away. With fingers that trembled, Joey went about the belated task of buttoning her blouse. That finished, she drew up her knees and folded her arms about her legs. Resting her forehead on her knees, she tried to gain hold of herself, constricting her eyelids to hold back the tears. But soon she was overcome by wrenching sobs, deploring her abandoned behavior with a man only too eager to take advantage of her weaknesses, and grieving for the ache deep within that knew no solace.

Chapter Seven

It was growing warm in the van with the bright sun beating in, and Joey lowered her window a bit to invite in more air. They had been driving nonstop for almost four hours now, and she was growing restless with anxiety. It seemed that they had been traveling forever across a dry region of endless chalk-colored hills and buttes. Certainly La Paz couldn't be too far off now, she thought wearily.

She glanced at the stony profile to her left. Mark seemed to be tiring, too, judging by the listless tedium conveyed in his pose. He was leaning to one side, his left arm carelessly draped over his opened window and his right hand casually hooked over the top of the steering wheel. His eyes were set on the road in a dour expression and he appeared engrossed in his own thoughts. She had no need to wonder what those thoughts must be.

He had said hardly a word and had been belligerent in manner ever since their terrible encounter of the day before. After storming out, he had returned to the van a few hours later and wordlessly drove them to a nearby trailer park where they had camped for the night.

He had prepared a fine dinner of the roosterfish he had caught, but neither of them appeared to be hungry enough to do it justice. After dinner he had lugged out his sleeping bag and spread it on the ground next to the van, leaving her the complete privacy of the vehicle. Then came the only time he had spoken to her the whole evening: As they were about to retire he ordered her to lock the door of the van from the inside. Even now she wondered at this unexpected admonition. But what difference did it make what his reasons were? They would soon be rid of each other.

She leaned her head against the high-backed seat and closed her eyes. After only a few moments, however, she found herself looking at Mark again from the corner of her eye. His smooth black hair and dark skin contrasted sharply with his white, navy-trimmed knit sport shirt. It emphasized his broad shoulders and clung to his muscular physique.

Yes, she had to admit he was handsome, as her eyes took in his well-defined profile, the firm jaw, and the thick straight hair that ruffled over the back of his collar. She sensed the quiet strength in the rhythmic rise and fall of his chest with each slow breath he took. Her lips parted slightly now, as her eyes traveled over his bared muscular forearms and strong, well-formed hands. Had those arms really held her . . . those hands caressed her body?

She winced and turned her head away to gaze blurry-eyed out the side window. It was suddenly too painful to study him. It hurt too much to be reminded of the wild emotions he had aroused in her—and to remember that he had only been trying to use her, that he was on his way to Cabo San Lucas and his mistress.

"What hotel are your parents staying at?"

The question, uttered in a monotone, cut through her consciousness. "What? Oh . . . the Hotel La Playa," she told him.

He gave a nod of recognition and continued to keep his eyes fixed on the winding road.

"Will . . . will we be in La Paz soon?" she asked, straightening up. She was not eager to speak to him, but was pressured by the anxiety of not knowing when this torturous ride would be over.

"You can see it ahead there," he told her, pointing briefly out the window. They had come to a high bluff which looked over a sweeping panorama of the Gulf of California and Bahia de La Paz. A cluster of tiny white buildings could be discerned on the far side of the bay where Mark had directed her attention. At last, La Paz was in sight! She breathed a silent, but long sigh of relief as the road led them on a sharp descent toward the coastal plain.

It was after a drive of another twenty miles or so along the bay when at last they came upon the city. Mark turned down a long entrance road leading to the hotel, which now loomed ahead. It was a tall, modern building of about a dozen stories, constructed of gray stone and situated on the beach of Bahia de La Paz.

Shortly they were in the hotel's parking lot, and as Mark looked for a space, Joey found her nerves incredibly on edge. Her fingers twisting about one another in anxiety, she silently wondered what the good-bye would be like. What would they say to one another? How would it finally end?

He parked, then went to the back of the van, took out her luggage and put it outside on the pavement. Heart beating rapidly, Joey went to pick up the bags.

"I'll take them for you," he said as he was locking up the vehicle. "The reception desk is upstairs."

She waited quietly and then they walked up a number of gray stone steps until they came to the modern, attractive lobby, which was only semi-enclosed and open to the

113

warm, tropical air. He set her bags down by the reception desk.

"Are a Mr. and Mrs. Ed Scott registered here?" he asked the girl behind the desk.

She checked her records. "Yes, they are—room four sixteen."

Mark nodded and turned to Joey, his eyes hard and his face grim. "I guess that's it then."

"Yes . . ." she replied in a barely audible voice, trying desperately to think of something to say.

"Good-bye." He had spoken the word before she quite realized it and all at once was walking away from her and back down the steps.

Suddenly remembering, she called out, "Mark, wait!" and ran down the few steps it took to reach him. He stopped and waited for her, his face expressionless, but his eyes strangely bright and expectant.

"I wanted to repay you," she said, reaching into her shoulderbag. She withdrew some Mexican currency and a sheet of notepaper, which she extended to him. "I made a list and added up my share of the expenses. I think you'll find it's all in order—and here's what I owe you."

He made no move to take the money she held out to him, but stared at her, his eyes reddening and his facial muscles tensing. "Haven't we come any further than the day we first met?" he said in a voice that was strained and harsh. "Are we still strangers to one another?"

"If you mean you expected to be repaid in some other way, I'm afraid you'll have to make do with the money," she said snappishly.

He drew his brows together as if in pain. "You don't owe me anything! Is doing something for someone else out of kindness a foreign concept to you? Don't you think it's possible I may have helped you just because I wanted to—because the reward was in the doing and not because

114

I expected something in return?" He studied her blank expression. "No, you don't understand that. You can't trust anyone enough not to question their motives. It's easier for you to deal with human emotion in business terms, so you quantify everything, reducing life to a list of debits and credits."

He stopped speaking and regarded her through taut, glassy eyes. "I feel sorry for you, Joey," he added in a quieter voice. "Unless you learn to trust people—including men—you're going to wind up a very lonely woman." He pushed aside her outstretched hand. "Keep your damn money. There's only one thing I'd ever accept from you, and you're not capable of giving it!" He turned and hurried down the steps without looking back. In a moment he was out of view, gone from her life.

Joey looked at the money still clutched in her tremorous hand, then down the steps to the spot where she last saw him. She opened her mouth as if to cry out, but found no words for her tongue to pronounce. Emptiness overcame her and she seemed at one with the cold stone steps on which she stood—dead inside.

"Jo? Jo—is that you?"

She heard a man's footsteps behind her and turned to face a gray-headed, middle-aged man of medium height and somewhat portly build. "Dad!" she cried, reawakening to her surroundings.

"Oh, thank God you got here all right! We've been so worried!" He gave her a strong embrace. "Jo, your mother has been so upset," he said, putting an arm about her and leading her slowly up the steps. "I haven't been out fishing since we got here! We heard about those heavy storms and the washouts, people stranded and whatnot—well, she's just been beside herself! I've had to stay close by and try to comfort her. I told her you had a good head on your shoulders and you'd make it through all right. I didn't let on, but I was worried, too."

They turned into the lobby and she pointed out her luggage, not wanting to interrupt. He picked up her bags and continued as they walked toward the elevator. "I didn't know what the road was like and about the trouble getting gas in some areas—I thought those were just stories. And then the storms! The weather was clear when we went through. I couldn't imagine driving through washouts; the potholes were bad enough. And we didn't know where you were—if you were stuck in the thick of the storms or had left later than we expected."

He paused a moment as they entered the elevator together. "Well, it's all my fault," he went on. "I should have waited for you at Estero Beach so you could have gone with us. I never thought it would be like this."

"That's okay, Dad. It wasn't so bad. I . . . I made it all right," she said, putting on a smile and hoping to ease his mind. She in fact was rather astounded. She had never seen her father in such a dither.

The elevator opened onto the fourth floor. "The room's this way," he said, quickening his pace as they walked along a flower-trimmed balcony overlooking the open air restaurant and the shimmering pool beyond. Farther out was the broad sandy beach and blue waters of the bay.

Joey wasn't sure, but it seemed to her that her father's hand shook a bit as he turned the key in the door to their room. "Milly!" he called as he opened the door and set the luggage down inside. "Milly, look who I found!" He brought Joey into the large, beautifully furnished room and pushed her forward, as if presenting her to his wife.

Her mother, still dressed in her robe though it was noontime, looked up from a book she was reading by the window. Her reddened eyes opened wide and in a moment

116

she was on her feet with her arms flung about her daughter. "Oh, thank heaven!" she gasped through her tears.

"I'm okay, Mother," Joey said softly, trying to soothe the slightly plump little woman who was clinging to her.

"We've been waiting so many days," her mother said, sniffing back her sobs. "I was afraid you drowned in one of those washouts!"

Joey smiled. "I didn't leave until Christmas Day and the storms were over when I went through. There was only one large washout where I was delayed for a few hours because a trailer got stuck."

Her father's expression was puzzled. "Then you should have made it here by yesterday, if not sooner," he said.

"Yes, well . . . I had a few other delays," Joey hedged.

"I'm sure it must have been very trying for you, dear," Joey's mother said with sympathy. "I should never have allowed this to happen. It's my fault—I should have insisted we wait for you at Estero Beach."

"No, no, Milly. It's my fault and I admit it. Don't blame yourself," Ed Scott told his wife.

"If I want to blame myself, I will!" the small woman quietly retorted as Joey's eyes widened. Mrs. Scott turned back to her daughter. "Now, tell me more about your trip, dear," she said, motioning for Joey to sit down on the edge of one of the room's two double beds. Milly took a place beside her, while Mr. Scott quietly took a chair by the window. "How did your little car hold up?"

Joey took a deep, slow breath. She would have to tell them sooner or later. "I'm afraid I got into an accident . . ."

"Oh, no!"

"Well, I wasn't hurt, Mother," she hurried to explain, "but my car is in Guerrero Negro being repaired."

"How did you get here?" her father asked with surprise.
She took another breath. "I . . . happened to meet

117

someone on the road—another American—and got a ride."

"Oh, that was nice! Who was it? A family on vacation?" her mother asked.

"No . . . uh . . . it was a man, traveling on his own in a van," she said, deciding to tell the whole story at once and get it over with.

"What?" her father reentered the conversation. "Oh, you mean it was some elderly man?"

"No, Dad, he was in his early thirties—and not married." She looked down at the carpet as she waited for the thunder to follow her lightning bolt.

"You took a ride in a van from some stranger!"

"What else was she to do in her predicament?" Milly Scott asked her husband crossly. "I'm sure she must have analyzed the situation first."

"But, Milly, she left her car in Guerrero Negro. A person can't make it from there to here in one day very easily." He turned his eyes back to Joey. "Didn't you have to spend the night somewhere?"

"Well, of course she would have stayed at a hotel—in her own room!" her mother explained with impatience.

"No, Mother, I spent the night with him in his van. In fact, I spent three nights camping with him." An icy silence followed her quiet statement.

"How dare you tell me that!" her father suddenly raged. "I didn't raise my daughter to go sleeping around with strangers!"

"Now just a minute," Mrs. Scott put in, her voice not quite so firm as before. "She didn't say she . . . was intimate with him. Besides that, she's of age—she doesn't owe us any explanations."

"The hell she doesn't. . . ."

"Mother's right. I don't owe you an explanation," she told her father sternly. "But I'll give you one, if you choose to believe it. Nothing happened between . . . between this man and me that you wouldn't approve of. He didn't touch me," she assured them, blanching the truth a bit. Since Mark was out of her life, it wouldn't matter anyway.

"I believe you, Joey," her mother assured her.

"Okay, Jo," her father said quietly. "You've never lied before; there's no reason to doubt you now. But it's hard to imagine—morals being what they are these days—that a young bachelor wouldn't try to take advantage of you. You are a beautiful girl, after all."

Joey lifted her eyes to her father's face. He had never before made any comment on her comely appearance. Her conscience suddenly bothering her, she said, "Well, he did seem to be attracted to me, but I didn't let him get very far."

"Good for you, Jo! I always said you could take care of yourself," her father vocally applauded. "Who was this guy anyway?"

Joey was quiet for a moment. "His name was Mark Chavira. He was from Orange County . . ."

"Chavira?" her father interrupted. "He wasn't a real estate developer, was he?"

"Yes, he . . ."

"You traveled with Mark Chavira?" he said with astonishment. "Are you sure? He's one of the most successful men in California—and becoming one of the richest! You must have seen him mentioned in the newspapers—the business and real estate sections?"

"I usually just have time to read the front page . . ." she weakly replied, stunned by her father's information.

"Well, he made the front page of *The Wall Street Journal* a few months ago. It was an article telling how he made his development company the most prominent in

Orange County before he was even thirty—and you know all the building that's been going on in that area. That man has such an instinct for buying property, it's uncanny. Boy, if I had had his ability . . ."

Joey's mind drifted from her father's voice to her own thoughts. No wonder Mark had always seemed so assured, so secure within himself that he could laugh at his own shortcomings. He was already so successful, he didn't need to impress anyone.

"Maybe you should have gone after him, Jo." The sound of her nickname broke her line of thought. "If you had snagged him for a husband, you could have been set for life."

"I don't want to be set for life," she told her father. "I'd rather rely on myself."

"Well, he's probably got more women after him than he knows what to do with, anyway," her father quipped, attempting to lightheartedly dismiss his previous comment.

"I imagine he does," Joey agreed sullenly.

"It doesn't matter how successful a man is," her mother put in unexpectedly. "It's what he's like to live with day in and day out that's most important!"

"Yeah . . . well . . ." her father said, clearing his throat and shifting about in his seat. "What do you say we three go to lunch downstairs. How about it?" he said brightly, as though trying to work up some enthusiasm for the idea.

"I suppose I *should* eat something," Joey said, not feeling very hungry.

"I'm not dressed yet. I've been so upset. Why don't you go with your father and I'll stay here and order a little something from room service."

"We'll wait for you, Milly," Ed Scott said eagerly.

"Of course, Mother," Joey agreed.

"No, I'd rather stay here, dear," she told Joey. "You go ahead."

Joey said no more to try to persuade her. It was clear something had changed between her parents and for the moment she thought it best to let matters alone. She said good-bye to her mother and followed her father to the restaurant downstairs. Here they were quickly seated at a small table.

They were silent for a few minutes after they ordered their sandwiches. Her father's enthusiasm had disappeared on the way downstairs and he now appeared depressed and worried. After absently pushing his glass and utensils about on his place mat, he at last said, "Well, I guess you've noticed I don't rate too highly with your mother lately."

"Yes, I . . ."

"I haven't seen her carry on this way in all the years we've been married," he continued. "She says I'm inconsiderate . . . that I always have my own way. Well, maybe she's right. I realize I did the wrong thing in asking you to drive here alone, and I admit it. By the way, I owe you an apology for that, Jo."

"That's okay, Dad."

"I've apologized to your mother, too, over and over. I never expected her to be so unforgiving."

"Maybe it's just because she was so worried. She'll probably be more herself now."

Ed Scott shook his head. "I don't know. She's hardly been speaking to me and refuses to eat with me. You can see that hasn't changed, even though you're back, safe and sound. And then last night,"—he grew visibly troubled and spoke more hesitantly—"she said something about . . . leaving me."

Joey felt herself growing pale. She never dreamed things could be this bad.

"I really don't know what to do, Jo. I can't see myself without her. I've been so contented all these years. She's always been there."

"Have you ever wondered if she was content?" Joey asked as gently as she could.

"She never said she wasn't," he replied, shrugging his shoulders.

"Well, I don't think she's ever thought much about herself. She was too busy taking care of us. Have you ever told her how much you appreciate her always being there for you?"

"Well . . ."

"Have you ever asked her what she would like to do for fun? Do you think she likes to sit around and amuse herself while you go off on your fishing trips?"

"But, Jo, she never complained," her father pointed out.

"Dad, I think she thought it was her duty as a wife to please you, so she went along with whatever you wanted." Joey desperately tried to think of some other way to get through to him. "Look, do you think Mother is an attractive woman?"

"Of course!" he readily answered. "She's certainly a lot prettier than other women her age. She was always beautiful."

"Yes, she is. Now don't you think it's possible other men have noticed her? If you don't appreciate her and spend some time seeing to it that she's happy, someone else might come along who's only too willing to give her the attention she needs."

"Oh, but your mother wouldn't—"

"Let me tell you something," Joey interrupted. "I tried to tell you this once before, but you were all up in the air over the whopper you had just caught. Last time we were at Estero Beach, when you were out fishing, a very polite and handsome middle-aged man—a widower, he said—spent the afternoon talking to Mother. He seemed very disappointed when she mentioned we were leaving the next day. And I think it was the most enjoyable day Mother had on that whole vacation."

"Is that true?" her father said, deeply shocked. "I never realized . . . I guess you're right, I'd better do something."

"You've already made a good beginning—giving up your fishing to be with her when she needed comfort," Joey pointed out optimistically. "Why don't you continue to spend more time with her and do things she would like to do. Take her shopping, sightseeing. Entertain her like you did when you were courting."

"But she won't even have lunch with me. I'll have to get out of the doghouse first."

Joey paused to think, as his point was well taken. "Maybe if I have a talk with her. I'll tell you what—why don't you go out and buy her something you think she'd like, some nice gift. Meanwhile I'll see if I can plead your case."

"I suppose it's worth a try," her father said with a long sigh.

Joey could tell how upset he was by the tone of his voice and his inability to finish his sandwich; his stocky figure attested to his usual appetite. Her eyes glazed over and she was touched. Perhaps men weren't so insensitive after all—some men, at any rate.

When Joey returned to the hotel room, she was relieved to see that her mother appeared to be more herself. She was dressed in pink slacks and a matching top; her short hair, softly frosted to hide the gray, was combed into its usual neatly attractive style. She was a lovely woman, Joey thought, a sweet face to match her usual temperament, a kindly smile, and though she carried a few extra pounds, they seemed to have distributed themselves to the right places. A light coat of makeup brightened the unusually pale complexion that Joey had noticed earlier.

"You look much better, Mother," she said brightly.

"Yes, I had a bite to eat and I feel better now that I know you're all right. How was your lunch?"

"Fine . . ." Joey hesitated, not knowing how to bring up the touchy subject. "I had a little talk with Dad. He was concerned that you've been so upset. He blamed himself."

"It *was* his fault," Mrs. Scott interrupted. "But it's mine, too. I . . . I should have said something more forceful than I did to make him wait for you at Estero Beach."

"Now, Mother, what could you have said? We both know how Dad is when he's set on something."

"Well, it's true he never listens much to my opinions; but this time I should have *made* him listen . . . somehow. There's no excuse for me not to take more responsibility than I do in our family," Milly said with newfound conviction. "I blamed him at first because he's always been inconsiderate when he's bent on following his own plans, but I'm beginning to see that it may be partly my fault that he's like that. I've always given in to please him. I thought I was being nice, but I see now that so much compliance can sometimes lead to trouble, even danger. I wouldn't have cared for myself, but my giving in to his wishes put you in danger. I should never have allowed that to happen," she finished, shaking her head in disapproval.

"Please don't blame yourself. It's nobody's fault. It just happened. Dad didn't realize the roads were that bad and no one could have predicted the rainstorms and floods. He's really sorry about it all. Why, he didn't eat even half of his lunch, he felt so bad."

"Good. He needs to lose weight," her mother commented tersely.

Joey was reluctant to press the subject further, but she felt constrained to do so. "Dad said something that

124

. . . well . . . that you had thought of leaving him." She found her voice failing her.

Milly Scott raised her eyes to her daughter's worried ones, then looked down. A little smile formed on her lips. "Yes, I guess I did. I was very upset last night. I was sure I'd never see you again. In my grief and anger I decided I didn't want to live with him anymore. I even made plans," she said, chuckling a bit. "I was going to move out, get my own apartment, like you have, and get a job. I was going to go back to school and study nursing in the evenings. You've always told me how you like being independent and unattached. Somehow I thought that was the thing that I should do."

"Are you?" Joey asked, holding her breath.

Mrs. Scott smiled again. "No, Joey. I've been married too long to change my life around. And in spite of your father's shortcomings, I guess I still love him. Besides, his life would fall apart without me, whether he realizes it or not," she added ruefully.

"I think he does," Joey said, relaxing now. "Being independent has its drawbacks anyway. I don't think you would have liked it."

Milly Scott's eyes widened a bit at Joey's words. "I'm surprised to hear you say that. You've never mentioned any drawbacks before."

"Well, *any* life-style will have some aspects that are less than perfect. Of course, *I* would certainly still prefer being single to being married," Joey said, sounding more like she was trying to convince herself than her mother of the firmness of her conviction, "but I have to admit that sometimes it does get a little . . . well . . . lonely. I don't think it would have suited someone like you, who's been living with a husband for so long."

"Sometimes you feel lonely?" Mrs. Scott asked with gentle concern. "When, for example?"

Joey hesitated before speaking and moved toward the window to look out onto the bay. "Oh, I remember one Saturday last spring. It was the first weekend I managed to have off from work after the tax season. It was a warm day and I guess I just got a case of spring fever."

"I thought you had gotten over those fits in your teens, when you used to be depressed because the young men you liked still looked upon you as a tomboy," her mother said with a kindly chuckle. "Tell me about it."

"Well, it was just a . . . a feeling. I was sort of restless and melancholy for no reason. There was a warm breeze that day and it was sunny—flowers all over. I went out and took a walk by myself. I saw pairs of lovers walking hand in hand, looking so happy. I felt . . . it was silly, but I felt lonely and romantic. I wished I had someone."

Joey was suddenly embarrassed, realizing her eyes were brimming with unshed tears. Quickly she blotted her eyes. "My goodness," she said with a self-conscious little laugh, "I guess the warm breezes here have afflicted me again."

Mrs. Scott studied her daughter, her expression a combination of wisdom and wonder. For a moment she looked as though she wanted to ask something, but then thought better of it and dropped her gaze thoughtfully to the floor.

"Anyway, Mother, I'm glad you're not really going to leave Dad. He may have his flaws, but he really loves you, you know."

Her mother raised her eyes to Joey's again and smiled. "I know."

"You'll have dinner with him tonight?" Joey asked hesitantly. "He said you had been refusing to eat with him."

"Of course. I'll have dinner with you both, I hope! I think my emotional outbursts are over with now," Mrs. Scott said, laughing a little at herself.

Joey smiled and gazed out again at the beautiful blue of

the bay, glad she no longer had to worry about the preservation of her parents' marriage.

After a few moments of silence, her mother suddenly asked, "Joey, do you think I'm too old to go back to studying nursing?"

"Too old! Why, of course not."

"Well, maybe I ought to go back to school and try it then. I've been thinking, perhaps I ought to do something that gets me out of the house a little more. I've had a lot of free time in these years since you left home."

Joey's eyes brightened immediately. "That's a wonderful idea! I think it would do you good to have some outside interest." She paused to think a moment and her gleeful expression faded. "I don't know how Dad would feel about it, though."

Mrs. Scott was very pensive for quite a while. At last she lifted her head and said, "I don't think it matters that much how he feels about it. Since I'll be the one with all the homework, it seems to me it's *my* decision to make."

A widening smile of surprise and satisfaction came over Joey's face. "You're absolutely right, Mother! It *is* your decision."

Chapter Eight

It was a kind of dull, listless day during the first week of the New Year. The morning sky was overcast and though the temperature was comfortable it was not quite warm enough to make swimming pleasurable. Joey took her usual lounge chair by one corner of the pool, the place she had occupied hour after hour every day since she had arrived.

Her parents—the love birds as she referred to them in her private thoughts—were off sightseeing again. Her mother had decided she wanted to see Land's End, the rocky southern tip of the Baja California peninsula at Cabo San Lucas, and Mr. Scott had eagerly complied with his wife's wishes, as he had ever since Joey had rejoined them.

As usual they had tried to coax Joey into coming with them, but she preferred to spend the day by herself again —to allow her parents time alone together, she rationalized. The fact was she had lost interest in seeing any more of Mexico and had shuddered at the suggestion she ac-

128

company them to Cabo San Lucas. She would be content never to see the popular resort in her life.

So, when her parents had left early that morning to make the more than three-hour drive to the tip of the peninsula, Joey had again donned her bikini, picked up her sun hat, beach robe, suntan lotion, and a few magazines and walked down to sit beside the pool. The previous days spent this way had been sunny, or at least partially sunny, and she had acquired a healthy-looking tan, having been careful to make use of her long beach robe and hat to cover herself when she felt she might be overdoing her exposure.

But though her stunning figure and glowing complexion made her look the picture of health, her eyes, hidden behind sunglasses, remained red-rimmed and forlorn.

She picked up a fashion magazine she had recently purchased and absently leafed through the pages, but as was usually the case, she soon found her mind was not on the latest modes from Paris or the newest beauty tips. Her thoughts, as always, traveled unerringly to Mark, to their final conversation, to the image of his tall figure as he stood before her predicting that she would become a lonely woman—a woman to whom life was nothing more than a list of debits and credits.

It couldn't be true, she told herself. She could feel; she had emotions, hadn't she? She was capable of love—she had loved! Only she had chosen badly.

Mark had said she needed to learn trust. But how could she trust men who had obviously tried to deceive her? First Robin and now Mark. Both had tried to make her believe that they had had no other women but her.

Of course she could have been wrong about Mark; she had no hard evidence against him. She hadn't actually caught him with another woman, as she had Robin. And Mark had seemed so sincere when he told her he had no one else, even appearing injured and insulted when she didn't believe him.

Now she regretted not having allowed him to explain. Maybe she had misunderstood the conversation she had overheard. And perhaps the beautiful girl in the photograph was a relative of his. She had lately recalled that Ted Morley used the term old lady when he referred to the woman in Cabo San Lucas that Mark was to pick up. Wasn't it possible he could have meant a woman who actually was of an older age—perhaps a mother or grandmother? Maybe she had been mistaken in assuming he was using the slang meaning of wife or mistress.

Still, she could not forget the sensually predatory way Mark had looked her over in Ensenada and Ted's careless remarks which indicated that he, at least, looked upon Mark as a womanizer on the prowl. After pursuing her so relentlessly, would Mark have left her as abruptly as he had if he really cared for her? Would a man with his self-confidence give up so easily if a woman were really special to him? No, she decided, tears forming in her eyes, if he had really cared he would have . . .

"Joey?" Her dolorous thoughts were interrupted by a hesitant male voice.

"Yes?" she said with a sniff, blinking to clear the tears from her eyes. "Oh, hello, Ray . . . Keith," she said, looking up to the two young men gazing down at her. Surreptitiously she wiped away a tear and put on a smile. "Nice to see you again."

"I'm glad to see you got here all right," Ray, the redheaded one who seemed to be more talkative, replied. "Is something wrong?" he asked solicitously, noticing a tear streaming down her other cheek from beneath her sunglasses.

"Oh, no," she assured him. "Just something in my eye. Have you been in La Paz all this time?"

"We spent a couple of days here and then went down to Cabo San Lucas. We're starting to head home now—just stopped here for lunch. Have you been staying at this hotel?"

"Yes."

"Must be nice," Keith put in with an envious smile. "We're getting a little tired of trailer parks."

"I know how you have to pinch pennies when you're a student," Joey sympathized. "How . . . how did you like Cabo San Lucas?"

"Oh, it was great!" Ray exclaimed, a broad smile breaking across his freckled face. "There are some guys on the beach there with big motorized rowboats. They take people out to see the offshore arches and rock formations at Land's End. We went out on one of the boats—saw pelicans and seals sunning themselves out there on the rocks. The arches were spectacular. It was really a neat place! Then we walked through the lobbies and grounds of some of the big resort hotels."

"That's all we could afford to do is walk through," Keith added with a laugh.

"Yeah," agreed Ray. "Maybe someday we'll be rich enough to stay at one of those places. Well, we'd better get going. We just came out here by the pool to take a look at the beach and happened to see you. I'm really glad we ran into you again. I was a little worried when we left you in Loreto. That guy you were with looked like he could be pretty tough if he wanted to be. And you didn't sound like you were too happy traveling with him."

"Oh, he was all right. He . . . he got me here safely," she said, struggling for words.

"That's good. I won't have that on my conscience anymore. Well, good luck! Enjoy the rest of your vacation!" Ray said, turning to go.

"Good-bye," Keith added with a wave.

She waved and watched them walk back toward the building until they disappeared into the lobby area. "I wish I could meet more fellows like them," she muttered. "Only a little older," she added ruefully. A man with a conscience! That was something unusual.

She wondered how much of a conscience Mark had. True, he had seen to it that she was safely deposited at her hotel, even though he was angry with her. And he wouldn't accept her money . . .

Her thoughts stopped as she recalled his parting words: "There's only one thing I'd ever accept from you, and you're not capable of giving it." What had he meant? What wasn't she capable of giving? Friendship? Love? Or was it just physical satisfaction he was looking for?

Oh, why think about it anymore? She'd go crazy if she did! With a restless movement she tossed her magazine and sunglasses aside and got up off of the chair. Turning about, she looked out from the raised pool area to the beach and bay below. Thinking some exercise might help straighten out her circular thought patterns, she put on her long white beach cover-up made of a thin gauzelike material and walked over to the flight of steps that led down to the broad, sand beach.

She walked all the way out to the water's edge and strolled alongside it, the waves gently lapping over her bare feet from time to time. Like a lost soul, her long hair and white garment blowing about her slender body in the breeze, she looked bleakly out to the far horizon, scanning the indistinct line that separated sky and sea. Even the elements, like her thoughts, were confused and ran together.

She looked up and noted that the cloud layer above was breaking, allowing scattered sunshine to come through. Perversely, she was disappointed. She preferred the gray dullness the morning sky had brought; it suited her clouded spirit. Sunshine had a way of making her feel lonely.

She walked to a point parallel to the hotel's edge and then turned around and began to stroll back the other way. She recalled her discussion with her mother about the way she had felt so lonely that warm, sunny Saturday a number of months ago. For the first time she had admitted aloud that being single, independent, and living alone were not keeping her as happy and carefree as she would have liked to believe.

During the first year she had her own apartment, when she started working after graduation from college, she had thought she could be happy with that mode of living forever. But the second year alone had not pleased her quite so much, and she found she was glad to be able to go to her old home to have her evening meals with her parents rather than to have to eat alone.

And now? If she were totally truthful with herself, she had to admit that she wasn't really happy at all. Her life consisted of work, sleep, meals with her parents, tennis, and occasional outings with the few girl friends she had left who were also still single. She was successful in her nascent career, but that was the only aspect of her life that brought her a sense of well-being.

She stopped and looked out to the horizon again as the sun broke through the clouds above her, suddenly bathing her in warmth and light. Her eyes became moist and her lips trembled. "It's true, I do . . . want . . . to be married," she whispered to herself, her tongue having difficulty in actually verbalizing the admission.

But after she had pronounced the words, a kind of peace stole over her, a release of tension quieting her quickened heartbeat, as though her troubled spirit had at last resolved its unbearable conflict.

She walked on a few more paces. After several minutes,

however, she sensed her brief euphoria gradually slipping away from her like the waves on the sand. She found that the idea of actually being married to a man was terribly frightening. Would it mean giving up her career? Would she lose all her autonomy? Would her own identity be completely absorbed into her husband's, never to be found again? Suddenly she was feeling she would rather go back to the idea of staying single.

"No, I don't want to do that," she told herself softly. "I can't stay like this. Oh, what's the matter with me? I'm afraid of being lonely and afraid of being married. I might as well be afraid of life!"

Angry with herself now, she walked on a few agitated paces, then stopped and looked up at the brightening sky. "I'll manage it somehow," she assured herself in a firm whisper, lowering her gaze to her own footsteps in the sand. "It'll take me a while to get used to the idea of marriage, to rethink my old attitudes, to find a man with whom I can share a mutual respect—a man I can trust and love." She watched as a wave flowed over her feet, then slipped away, carrying with it the very footprints she had been contemplating. She took a shallow, shuddering breath. "Oh, Mark, Mark," she moaned, her voice barely audible, "why couldn't it have been you? Why . . . ?"

"Do you always go about whispering things to yourself?"

The low, sardonic voice went through her like a shock wave. She swung around to face a very real Mark Chavira staring down at her, the ephemeral image she had been carrying suddenly turned into flesh and blood. Her mouth parted slightly as her eyes, huge with wonder, looked wistfully over his handsome features. His black hair mussed from the strong breeze, his skin tone deepened by recent exposure to the sun, he studied her face through dark eyes that burned with hard, anxious questions.

As she returned his gaze, she was unaware of the large wave that rolled over her feet, suddenly undermining the sand beneath her. He reached out and put his hands on her upper arms to steady her balance, then pulled her farther back onto the beach. When they had stepped back onto dry sand, he stopped, but she continued to move forward until she was against him, slipping her arms about his waist and resting her head below his shoulder.

He seemed momentarily stunned but soon encircled her in his arms and drew her even closer. "Well!" he exclaimed somewhat breathlessly. "To what do I owe this honor?" She looked up at him with tears flowing down her cheeks, her throat so tight with emotion she could not speak. His expression softened and lights danced in his eyes. "Don't tell me you actually missed me!"

"Yes," she whispered, taking in an uneven breath.

"Did you? You mean it? That's more than I'd even hoped for," he said softly, drawing her close against him once more.

He's back! He came back for me! her heart chimed. Then, suddenly anxious to be reassured, she asked, "What brings you to La Paz? Are you on your way home?" the thought coming to mind that he might just be passing through as Ray and Keith had been.

"No, I'm returning to Cabo San Lucas tomorrow. I came here today to . . . to tell you that I'll let you pay me back after all."

"Oh," she said, her heart beginning to sink.

"You can buy me a drink at the hotel's disco tonight," he told her with a smile.

Her mouth forced a faint answering smile. "Okay," she replied, as she felt herself tumbling back to earth.

They began to walk along the shore together as Mark studied her downcast demeanor. "What's wrong?" he

135

asked, brushing back the long windblown hair from one side of her face. "Don't you like discos?"

"They're all right, I guess," she replied. She hesitated, then decided to ask the question that troubled her mind. She stopped walking and turned to face him. "Mark, what did you mean when you said there was only one thing you'd ever accept from me? I . . . I didn't think you meant my buying you a drink," she said with a nervous smile.

His expression became grave. "No, I didn't." He grew quiet and began walking again with slow strides, his eyes on the sand in front of him.

She followed. "What did you mean then?" she asked with jittery persistence.

He stopped and looked down at her. His eyes seemed at once determined and apprehensive. "Joey, I'm in love with you. What I wanted—what I still want—is your love." He lowered his eyes to the sand, ". . . that is if you think you *can* love me."

Joey was speechless for a moment, afraid to believe her ears. Then she gushed, "Oh, Mark, I can and I do love you!" as she was throwing her arms about his neck, her heart joyously pounding with complete happiness. "I do love you!" she repeated, her cheek against his tanned neck, left bare by his open shirt collar. She pressed her lips against the warm skin and felt his strong arms constricting about her waist. "Mark," she gasped, raising her lips to invite his kiss. He took her mouth ardently with his own, pressing her tightly against him.

After a long while they breathlessly loosened their holds, smiling, even laughing a bit at themselves. Putting an arm about one another they began to walk slowly along the water's edge, dodging the waves and playfully pulling each other off balance. They were behaving just like all the pairs of lovers Joey had observed walking along the beach, she thought, as she nuzzled against Mark's shoulder.

"Why didn't you tell me you loved me before?" she asked.

"With you calling me every name in the book at any opportunity? I think I told you that I cared, but you were always so suspicious."

"I know, Mark. I'm sorry. I shouldn't have doubted you," she told him earnestly. "I know now that you were sincere."

"Are you sure?" he said with a smile, his eyes pinning her down. "I thought you had me down as a roguish skirt chaser. What about my other woman in Cabo San Lucas?"

"Oh, please don't talk about it," she begged, deeply ashamed. "I guess I just have a vivid imagination, blowing mistaken impressions all out of proportion. I've been leery of men for so long, it's probably distorted my thinking. I hope I'm cured now."

"With the bad experiences you've had, it's understandable," he said, giving her a comforting hug. "If there's anything you'd like me to explain . . ."

"No," she said firmly, her hand making a horizontal motion in the air. "I don't want you to explain anything. You've come back for me and that's all I need to know. You wouldn't have bothered if you'd had all those other women I was imagining."

"Good God, how many did you think I had?" he asked, much amused.

"Oh, hundreds!" she exclaimed, laughing at herself.

"I didn't know I had such a macho image," he said, raising his brows, while his eyes momentarily held a worldly, dissipated look.

"Oh, yes," she breathed, edging close to him. "That's why I was so afraid of you. I sensed you were more than I could handle. I was right!"

He chuckled silently. "Because I tracked you down and kept you prisoner in my van?"

"No," she said, laughing. "I thought I could be happy without a man, and you proved I was wrong."

"Taming an independent woman—I suppose that is sort of a macho-style accomplishment, at that," he said, looking rather satisfied with himself. He turned and looked into her eyes. "But Joey, I want you to realize that I'm really pretty soft-hearted underneath. I don't want you to think that I fit the image of an unbending, unemotional male. You said I was insensitive and . . ."

"And I was wrong. I know now you aren't." She glanced up at him and smiled. "You forgot to say you're also patient and forgiving. You must be to put up with me!"

"That's true," he agreed with mock conceit, then his eyes grew tender. "But you're worth it!"

They exchanged an affectionate kiss and, arms about one another, began to walk slowly back toward the hotel. "By the way," Joey said as they were climbing the steps to the pool area, "how come you didn't tell me you were rich and famous?"

"I'm rich and famous?" he responded with raised brows.

"My father knew you by name, said that you've been written up in all the papers, and that you're one of the most prominent businessmen in California."

Mark took a breath. "My company has been doing well, it's true . . ." he understated.

"Tell me how you accomplished it," she said eagerly, taking him by the arm. They had reached the top of the steps and she led him past the pool to some comfortable seats by the open-air bar. "Don't be modest. I want to know everything!"

"There's not that much to tell. I went to college, studied business and real estate, then went out and applied myself," he said, matter-of-factly.

"Just like that, huh?" she said, snapping her fingers.

"Well, it took a little time." he granted.

"And a little genius! Don't be so evasive. I understand business matters, or have you forgotten?"

His mouth formed a little smile while his eyes traveled knowingly from her childlike face with its small, turned-up nose and adorably pouting mouth to the brief but well-filled bikini discernible beneath her thin cover-up. "I do tend to forget that from time to time," he admitted.

She lowered her eyes and smiled, having thoroughly enjoyed his perusal. "So tell me about your career," she resumed her prodding. "I've been remiss in reading the newspapers regularly, so you'll have to fill me in on everything from your very first project to all your latest developments."

"That'll take all afternoon!"

"You have something better to do?" she sassed with a charming pout.

Mark made a wry face. "I see now how you get production from your difficult clients!"

They spent the next few hours talking leisurely over drinks and a late lunch at the outdoor restaurant while Mark outlined the history of the notoriously successful company he had founded. Joey asked many pertinent questions which he seemed only too happy to answer, his eyes taking on a certain pride as each of her queries reflected her keen business mind.

They were sitting by the pool late in the afternoon when Ed and Milly Scott returned from their day-long excursion. They approached the young couple and introductions were made and a cordial conversation ensued, accented by a profusion of thank-yous from Joey's parents for her safe deliverance and Mark's engaging efforts to secure their goodwill in return. In fact, the three were so predisposed to like one another, it almost made Joey uneasy.

"He's such a fine young man. So handsome, too," her mother was saying when Joey and her parents were back in their room. They were changing to have dinner with Mark at another hotel in the heart of La Paz.

"Oh, Mark's a great guy," her father agreed, as he was tying his tie before the mirror. "Any time you want to walk down the aisle with him is fine with me, Jo."

"What?" Joey gasped.

"Now, Ed, don't rush her. They haven't known each other long," her mother gently chided.

"If you ask me," Mr. Scott said omnisciently, "he's got his mind made up already!"

"But maybe Joey doesn't," his wife pointed out.

He turned away from the mirror and looked directly at his daughter. "Now, Jo, you don't want to pass him up." He broke into a smile. "I know, you women like to play hard to get. But it's obvious you two are crazy about each other, so there's no use being coy."

"I'm not, Dad," Joey objected, her thoughts suddenly confused. She loved Mark and only that morning had decided she wanted to be married, so why was she feeling panicky listening to this conversation?

"Sometimes these things take time, Ed. There's no need to force the issue. It's a matter to be handled between them alone, and I'm sure everything will fall into place in due course. Let's not embarrass Joey with any more conjecturing. And I don't want to hear any broad hints over dinner!" Milly Scott told her husband firmly.

Joey relaxed a bit at her mother's soothing words. Things were just happening a little too fast, that was all. There was a long step between deciding in theory to marry and actually marrying one man in particular. She realized her old fears were still lingering and she would need some time to exorcise them. Besides, Mark would be there to help her make all the adjustments, she thought, as a smile crept over her face.

Her mood suddenly carefree, she walked over to the mirror her father had just vacated to apply some makeup. Her complexion was so radiant, she found she needed very little. She combed her hair and checked her dress, a stylish, rose-colored garment with bouffant sleeves gathered at the wrists. It buttoned up the front to a high collar and its full skirt accentuated her small waist.

They met Mark in the lobby and drove together into town to a stately old hotel on a busy street which edged the waterfront. In the hotel's restaurant, they were seated at a heavy wooden table set beside a large window overlooking the bay. Joey found that conversation was easily maintained by her parents and Mark as they enjoyed their delicious fresh fish dinners.

"You mentioned this afternoon that you visited Cabo San Lucas," Mark was saying to the Scotts. "How did you like it?"

"Great place!" her father exclaimed. "And Milly liked it so much she was even willing to get into a boat to see Land's End!"

"Really?" said Joey with surprise, knowing her mother's fear of water and her tendency toward seasickness.

"Oh, your father did some of his fast talking to get me into one of those rowboats—that's all they were, you know. So off we went, farther and farther away from the beach, to see the huge rock formations. I was petrified, of course, but once we got back on shore, I was glad I went. It was very beautiful and majestic."

"I wish I had seen it, now," Joey said, recalling similar glowing reports from Ray and Keith.

"Would you like to?" Mark asked eagerly. "Actually, I was going to invite you all to come to Cabo tomorrow

141

to meet some of my relatives who own a restaurant there. But you may not feel like making the long trip again so soon . . ." he said, now addressing himself mainly to the elder Scotts.

Milly Scott's face brightened. "I wouldn't mind. Oh, I forgot, I promised Ed he could spend the day fishing," she said, turning to her husband. "He's been so good about taking me around," she explained, "I decided to let him get in some of the fishing he was so anxious to do. He signed up to go out tomorrow morning." -

"Oh, I guess I could skip it," Mr. Scott said a trifle reluctantly.

"No, I've heard how much you enjoy fishing. I do too," Mark sympathized jovially. "As long as you're here I wouldn't want you to miss it; La Paz is an ideal fishing area. Perhaps you wouldn't mind if your wife and daughter came out on their own?"

"Now that's a good idea!" Ed Scott said with enthusiasm. "You and Jo could take our car," he said to his wife. "It was a nice drive and the road wasn't bad. What do you think?"

"I'd love to if Joey is willing," Mrs. Scott responded, looking toward her daughter.

"Oh, sure," Joey replied, bewildered by the sudden turn of events. The idea of meeting Mark's relatives took her by surprise. "Should . . . should we follow you when you leave tomorrow?" she asked the handsome man sitting next to her.

"Well, you can if you want to get up at the crack of dawn. I promised my uncles I would be back bright and early to help them out. You see, they've been putting on an addition to the restaurant and they're running a little behind schedule. There's going to be a wedding in the family in a few days and the place was supposed to be ready for a party afterward. I've been helping out with

142

painting and putting the place in order. There's a lot to do even though the basic construction work is finished," Mark explained.

"After today I don't think I'd be able to get up that early," Mrs. Scott said with a smile. "I think it would be best if we left later in the morning, don't you, Joey?"

Her daughter readily agreed, not wanting to be in a position to spend the entire day with his relatives—a possibility which made her uneasy. She wondered what they would make of Mark's bringing her and her mother around to meet them. They might be as quick to jump to conclusions as her parents were. She told Mark they would arrive at about one or two o'clock in the afternoon.

After dinner they took a stroll down the palm-lined walk along the water's edge. It was a beautiful, clear evening and the air was warm and calm. Streetlights gave the city a soft glow as cars and pedestrians moved about, and offshore a few boats and ships of varying sizes were silently moored.

"Say, Mark, am I mistaken, or was there a write-up about your home in one of the local California magazines some time ago?" Mr. Scott turned to ask, as they walked in pairs, the Scotts taking the lead.

"Yes, there was. It was right after I had had it built and the interior designers were finished with their work," Mark told him.

"Looked like a beautiful home," Mr. Scott commented with the air of the experienced realtor that he was. "How many rooms?"

"Oh, let's see: six bedrooms, four bathrooms, two living rooms, dining room, breakfast room, office, den, game room, library, and . . . oh, yes, the kitchen. Of course there's a pool, and also a specially constructed outdoor barbecue. I've been thinking of adding a tennis court."

143

As Joey's head spun with this lengthy enumeration, her mother quipped, "Don't you get lost in all that space?"

"It has been a great deal more house than I need," Mark admitted, "but I built it with an eye toward selling it someday, unless, of course, things change," he added, turning his eyes on his lovely companion.

Joey glanced up at his intent, dark eyes and quickly looked away. The thought of being put in charge of running such a house was more than she could handle at the moment. She felt Mark take her hand and sensed his eyes were seeking hers again, but she dared not look up at him. A claustrophobic feeling began to overcome her and she fought the urge to escape.

Mark put an arm around her shoulders and gave her a little shake. With his free hand, he turned her head to look at him. His eyes were filled with amusement and understanding, as though he had read her mind and was silently chiding her for making a mountain out of a molehill. She smiled back, realizing that was exactly what she was doing, embarrassed now at her habit of escalating fears all out of proportion to reality. Suddenly she felt exuberant and lovingly slipped an arm about Mark's waist, under his sport coat. He was so good for her, she thought, marveling at his sensitivity to her emotional needs.

When they all had had enough walking, they drove back to the La Playa. Joey's parents graciously excused themselves to retire, saying it was already later than they usually stayed up, and encouraged the younger couple to go to the disco as they had planned.

"Do you think your parents like me?" Mark asked, as they were walking past the outdoor lobby to the entrance of the disco.

"Like you! They've practically been falling all over you," Joey exclaimed with a touch of asperity.

"I thought they seemed to like me, but with the questionable circumstances of our meeting and traveling together, I wouldn't blame them if they were a little dubious."

"They were when I first told them the story, but I explained that it was all perfectly innocent. And when my father found out who you were, you were completely exonerated."

"So they take me to be a proper gentleman?"

"Yes. Well, you are . . . more or less," she said with a sly grin.

He regarded her expression with amusement. "I'll have you know it wasn't easy, young lady. Why do you think I slept outside that last night? After our encounter earlier in the day, I couldn't trust myself anymore."

"So that was why you told me to lock the door. I thought maybe it was to prevent you from wringing my neck."

"That was my second reason," he sallied, trying to maintain a straight face.

As they neared the entrance to the disco, Joey looked out to the pool area, curious to see if it was being used. There was one lone swimmer in the water.

"It's kind of late to be swimming," she commented, looking back to Mark.

It seemed he hadn't heard her, his attention being completely engrossed in the attire of a young woman entering the disco with her escort. The attractive girl was wearing a clinging dress which uncovered more than covered her smashing figure. Joey and Mark watched together as she disappeared behind the door.

"Wow!" she heard Mark gasp under his breath before he turned to Joey with, "Did you say something?"

"Oh, it wasn't very important," she said in an airy but clearly injured tone of voice.

"Did you expect me not to notice her?" he said, correctly interpreting her reaction.

"Well, you didn't have to gawk. She's obviously just trying to attract attention to herself."

"Now, Joey, you know how men are. There'd be something wrong with me if I didn't look. It doesn't mean anything."

"How come you don't stare at me then? My figure's just as good as hers," she said in a slightly provocative manner.

There was a comfortable look in his eye as he replied, "Your figure is better. But at the moment it's not so much on display."

"And you're forced to look for the ones that are," she finished.

"Joey . . ." His voice was edged with exasperation.

"We'd better go in," she said, smiling to herself as she opened the door to the disco. She was glad she had managed to unsettle his calm attitude over the matter. Though her former misgivings about men were softening, she still felt men should be made to pay for their errant ways.

They entered the dimly lit room and found a small table just vacated near the crowded dance floor. Joey's spirits drooped a little as she picked out a few other well-proportioned young women in stylishly skimpy attire jiggling about on the dance floor. She looked at Mark and was both amused and miffed to see his surreptitious glances in their direction. She began to feel dowdy and schoolmarm-ish in her high-buttoned dress.

"Would you excuse me for a moment?" she asked Mark quietly before running off to the ladies' room.

When Joey returned a few minutes later to take her seat next to Mark, her appearance was somewhat altered. The buttons down the front of her dress from her collar almost to her waist were all undone, subtly revealing the smooth skin and shadowy, well-formed curves beneath.

Mark's startled expression instantly turned grim. "What have you done!"

Surprised at his reaction, she replied, "This is the way models wear their clothes in fashion magazines. Besides, I have to compete with all these other women for your attention."

"Will you sit up straight!" he ordered, glancing about at other men nearby. "You don't have to compete with anyone."

She complied by straightening her posture. "Come on now, you haven't missed one woman here in a low-cut dress. What's wrong with my wanting you to notice me, too?"

"Joey, I don't want all the men in here leering at you."

"You mean it's all right for you to ogle other women, but no one is supposed to look at me?"

"Right!" he said obstinately. "Now, will you button yourself up?"

"No!"

"Joey . . ."

"No!" she repeated, her expression as mulish as his.

"All right, young lady!" he said as he grabbed her tightly by the wrist, forcing her to rise from her seat. He pulled her by the arm relentlessly, passing curious onlookers, until they were through the door and outside again.

"How dare you!" she cried as she rubbed the bruised wrist he had at last released.

"No wife of mine is going to appear that way in public!" he stormed.

"I'm not your wife!" she retorted with a quivering lip.

Her statement made him pause. His dark eyes studied her for a moment, then slowly lowered to the ground. "You know I want you to be," he said quietly.

147

She swallowed convulsively. "W-why would I want to marry anyone who orders me around?" she asked in a small voice that seemed to cut through the night air.

His expression became troubled. "I'm sorry," he said, taking her hands in his. "I shouldn't have been so boorish, but I just couldn't tolerate the thought of other men eyeing what belongs to me, as if you were still on the market."

"You have no right to speak of me as if I were a piece of property you owned!"

"I didn't mean it to sound like that," he amended hastily. "I—" Mark was interrupted by a large group of people leaving the disco, who were forced to dodge them as they stood by the door. Mark pulled her away. "Why don't we go up to the top floor and see if there's a view," he suggested. "Maybe we can be alone there."

She nodded her acquiescence and they proceeded to take the elevator up to the top of the building. They walked out onto the empty balcony, past a number of hotel rooms, until they reached the end. "I guess it's too dark to see much," he said, looking out over the bay, "but at least we shouldn't be bothered." He took her hands again and looked down at her face. "Look, maybe I am possessive about you," he said, resuming their previous topic, "but that's the way a man behaves when he's in love and unsure of the woman he cares about. I like to think of you as mine."

"But . . . but I'm not. I don't belong to anyone," she asserted, suddenly finding her independence very precious.

His brows drew together. "You don't realize how much it hurts me to hear you say that. Don't I mean anything to you?"

The question threw her into confusion. "Yes, of course you do," she whispered.

"Do you still love me?"

"Yes."

He smiled, as if it were all so simple. "Then you belong to me, just as I belong to you—don't you see?"

She was deeply troubled and could not form a response. He enfolded her in warm, comforting arms. "Joey, is it making a commitment that frightens you so?" he asked softly. "Or are you afraid I'll take away your freedom and police your life, even tell you what you can and can't wear?"

"Yes!" she whispered.

"You're afraid I'll be one of those domineering men, like your father, perhaps, who'll only allow you to say yes, sir?"

She nodded her head.

"Well, I won't," he said, giving her a shake by the shoulders. "As long as you stay away from wearing plunging necklines in public, I'd want you to feel free to wear and do whatever you'd like. And your father didn't seem so high-handed as you described him. Is he really that bad?"

Feeling somewhat reassured, Joey made a little smile. "My mother's beginning to bring him under control."

"Good for her! Now, if your mother can do it, do you really have doubts about your ability to keep *me* in line?"

"Maybe you're right. She's managed to turn him to jelly lately," she replied, laughing a bit now as her fears began to ebb.

"It's not so hard," Mark said without joining in her amusement. "I feel like I've been losing my grip ever since I met you. You're the most unmanageable, unpredictable woman I ever saw. It's like trying to capture a butterfly— you always flit off in some unexpected direction. Don't run away from me anymore, Joey," he whispered, pressing her closer and lowering his mouth to hers.

She willingly succumbed to his hard embrace, putting

her arms around his neck and eagerly returning his kiss. His hands moved restively over her back, tangling in her long, silky hair.

"Say you'll be mine, Joey. Say you'll marry me," he prodded in a soft, urgent voice. "Will you?" His dark eyes riveted on hers through the dim light, expectant and impatient.

She stared back at him wide-eyed and unblinking for a long, suspended moment, knowing how much her future weighed upon her answer, but somehow unable to feel it. All the intuitive senses and emotions she usually relied upon suddenly had left her and her mind seemed strangely dulled. The dark eyes fixed upon her were growing more bleak with each fraction of a second she hesitated. All she knew now was that she couldn't bear to make him unhappy. "Yes," she responded in a tiny whisper.

His eyes became liquid and shimmering. "Joey," Mark said in an uneven voice, "I'll try to make you happy. You won't regret it." His arms tightened around her. She felt numb, as if her head and body were made of cotton, like a stuffed doll. But as he kissed her again, her vital, human force returned with increased strength, making her doubly sensitive to the feel of his hands and lips. She soon became lost in the warmth and darkness of his arms, wishing never to be found.

She felt Mark pulling away before she wanted to end the kiss. Rising up on tiptoes, she sought his lips again, but he restrained her. "There are some people coming," he told her quietly and then she became aware of the footsteps and soft conversation behind her. Feeling a little foolish, she drew away from him to a more decorous distance.

In another minute she heard a door close. "They're gone now," Mark told her with a smile. He took a step toward her and put his hands at her waist. "Where were we?"

Her small hands rose to the back of his neck and pulled him toward her. This time their kiss was immediately intense, as though a fiery electric current were passing between them. His hands moved roughly over her, soon finding the loose front opening of her dress, while his lips grew more demanding. The sensation of his long fingers moving caressingly over her soft, sensitive skin created an aching, a frightfully urgent desire within. Her breathing growing unsteady and her heart pounding, she clung to him, wanting more . . . more. . . .

Joey had barely heard the first distant burst of laughter. It came again, closer now, accompanied by the unwelcome sound of more footsteps at the other end of the balcony. Mark reluctantly took his mouth from hers, but they did not pull apart this time; it would have been too painful. He dropped his hands to her waist and inclined his head toward hers until the noisy couple approaching had found their room and gone in, shutting the door behind them.

Mark lifted his eyes to hers and they looked at one another with sadness and longing. "Busy place," he remarked, making an effort to smile.

"Mark, couldn't we go to your room? We could be alone," she said, her voice fading as she saw the pain in his eyes.

He slowly shook his head. "Do you know what you're asking? If you came with me to my room, you wouldn't leave until morning. I wouldn't have enough will power to let you go. I barely have enough now. Do you want to have to explain to your parents where you were all night? With the upbringing they've given you, would you feel right about it yourself?"

Joey bowed her head. "No," she admitted through quivering lips, tears forming in her eyes.

"Besides, you've had doubts about me, unfounded doubts, but apparently very real. I don't want to give you any reason to question the sincerity of my intentions toward you. You might willingly let yourself be carried away tonight and then feel tomorrow, in the cold light of day, that you had been used. I would rather wait until you're my wife and can come to me with complete trust than take any chances of reawakening your doubts."

She put her arms around his waist and buried her face in his chest. "Oh, Mark, I trust you. I don't know how I could have ever doubted you. But you're right," she said, pulling away, "it would be better not to . . . be alone with you. I didn't realize what I was saying."

"No, I don't think you did," he said, smiling down as he dried her eyes. "It's probably a good thing you've kept your distance from men all this time. I think you could be seduced very easily."

"Only by you," she amended with a pout.

"Good. I'll take you to your room now. I have to get up early anyway," he said, putting an arm about her and leading her back toward the elevator. "And you'd better button up that dress in case your parents are still awake."

"Okay," she softly replied as she dutifully started the chore. She smiled and a warmth stole over her. Mark was too good for her, she decided, happily noting that this was a statement she had always doubted she could make about any man.

Chapter Nine

It was a bright sunny morning as Joey and Milly Scott drove along Highway 1 toward Cabo San Lucas, passing through a dry, hilly landscape with the now-familiar desert vegetation. Joey blinked her eyes hard, feeling tired from not having slept well the night before. They had left much earlier than expected. Her mother, who apparently hadn't needed as much sleep as she had anticipated, had awakened early and hurried Joey along, anxious to be off.

"It will be nice to meet Mark's relatives, won't it, dear?"

"Oh, sure," Joey replied, gripping the steering wheel more tightly and wishing she hadn't been reminded of their reason for making the trip.

"What an advantage to have relations to visit in Cabo San Lucas! Just think, if you married Mark. Oh, I'm sorry. I didn't mean to sound pushy," Milly said, noticing her daughter's edgy reaction to the mention of marriage. "It's just that Mark is such a fine person and he seems so taken with you. In fact I thought I heard him drop a hint or two. I think you should begin to prepare yourself for a proposal, Joey."

"He . . . he did propose, Mother."

"He did!"

"Last night."

"What did you say?" her mother asked, breathless.

"I said yes. At least I think that's what I said. I'm sure that's what I said."

"You don't remember?" Mrs. Scott asked incredulously.

Joey briefly raised a tremulous hand to her forehead. "Well, it happened so fast . . . my mind was in a whirl. I felt pretty good about the whole idea when I came in and went to bed, but I woke up a few hours later in a panic. It was dark, and I felt, well, jittery and . . . and trapped. I kept going over what he and I said to each other, turning the words about in my mind, until after a while, I wasn't sure anymore what I told him. I suppose I was hoping I had really said, 'Let me think about it.' Things are clearer this morning, and I feel a little more secure again. I love Mark, but getting married is scary!"

"It is a big change in one's life," her mother agreed, a little troubled over her daughter's misgivings. "He probably just took you too much by storm. I'm sure you'll feel better about it soon."

"You know that I had always thought I would stay single. I never saw any advantage to being married," Joey explained. "Although I was lonely being unattached . . ." she admitted, reminding herself of that troublesome fact. "Now, within two weeks of meeting Mark, I'm engaged!"

Milly smiled sympathetically. "That isn't much time. He's obviously in a hurry, but maybe you could talk him into a period of engagement—perhaps a few months. That would give you some time to get used to the idea before actually taking the plunge."

"That may be a good idea! I hadn't thought of that,"

Joey exclaimed, her spirits suddenly lifting. "I could use the busy season as an excuse. In fact, I don't see how I could make any wedding plans until the tax season is over in the spring. I'll have to begin working overtime as soon as I get back. That would give me a few months to adjust," she said, mentally contemplating how well everything could fall into place. "If I still wasn't sure by that time, I could drag out making the wedding plans. . . ."

"Joey, it's his wedding, too. He might want to dash you off to Las Vegas, in which case there wouldn't be any plans to take your time with," her mother pointed out, bursting Joey's comfortable bubble of procrastination.

"Then I . . . I'd just refuse to go," she said, her apprehensions returning.

"I'm sure he wouldn't do anything that would make you unhappy," her mother reassured her. "I imagine he'd be willing to wait for a reasonable time since you haven't known each other long, but I don't think he'd let you get away with continually putting the date off. You'll have to face it sometime, Joey, or you may lose him. All changes in life are a little frightening, but if you don't go through them, you don't progress. I've been learning that myself."

"Yes, I suppose you're right," Joey agreed reluctantly.

"I know you're very much in love with him—you were miserable until he came back yesterday. Do you want to risk having that empty feeling for the rest of your life, just because you were afraid to give marriage a chance?"

"No," Joey replied in a forlorn voice. "But, Mother, what if I'm not happy being married. I know you're different from me, but I don't think I'd be content with the domestic life-style you've had."

"Well, I don't know that I've been entirely content with it myself," her mother admitted. "But you have a different temperament than I, so your marriage would probably be different as well. Also, Mark seems a little more perceptive than your father is about some matters. I don't see why you and Mark shouldn't be able to work things out together to suit yourselves."

"I hope so," Joey said with a worried sigh.

Soon they were entering the growing resort town of Cabo San Lucas, fronting a small harbor at the southernmost tip of Baja California. It was smaller than La Paz and not so well developed; more a sleepy village when compared to the urban center that was La Paz. But in the distance could be seen modern, elegant resort hotels, overlooking huge sandy beaches and the sea, which accommodated hundreds of tourists from many parts of the world.

Following the directions Mark had given them at dinner, Joey drove up to a pleasant looking, well-kept, low building marked RESTAURANTE. There were tables outside as well as inside, but there were no customers and the place did not appear to be open for business. Off to the side there was evidence of recent construction with lumber and building equipment lying around. It was about 10:30 in the morning as Joey parked the car in front of the building.

"I guess this is the place," Joey said, trepidation showing in her voice. "I'll bet it's not open yet. We're awfully early."

"Maybe they're inside. Why don't you go in and see?" her mother urged.

Joey was hesitant. "I feel kind of funny about this. I mean, Mark wasn't expecting us until this afternoon."

"Joey, we drove all this way to see him. I'm sure he won't mind if we're early. What makes you so diffident all of a sudden?"

"Meeting his relatives, I guess," she answered truthfully. "I tend to look at it as bringing me that much closer to the altar."

Her mother laughed. "Simply meeting his uncles and-cousins doesn't seal your future. Just take things one step at a time. Meanwhile, you have the love of a man a lot of women would give their eye teeth for, so try to be happy about it!"

"All right, Mother. Thanks," Joey said with a little smile, somewhat reassured by her calm good sense. She got out of the car and walked across the small street toward the restaurant. As she approached, she could see through a window that there were a few people inside the building, apparently putting the place in order. They appeared to be older—a woman and two men. Joey guessed the two men would be Mark's uncles. Suddenly she felt very uneasy. She hated to go and knock on the door asking for Mark, and thus cause them to speculate about her identity and reason for calling. She quickly decided it would be much better if she could simply locate him on her own without bothering his relatives. Besides, she rationalized, they may not speak English anyway.

Joey turned from her path toward the front entrance and followed the building around to the side, toward what appeared to be the newly constructed addition. Carefully stepping over some pieces of lumber lying on the sandy ground, she at last came to an open doorway and, stepping up to it, peered in.

She was not at all prepared for the scene that met her eyes. There, a short way inside, was Mark standing with his arms about a very beautiful, black-haired young girl. The girl in the picture! He was hugging her tightly and smiling down at her, while she, in turn, was raising her arms to encircle his neck and stretching up to kiss him.

Joey's heart seemed to stop. For a moment she turned to stone, her stunned eyes taking in the embracing couple —the lovely young Mexican girl, her slender body leaning against Mark's as she affectionately kissed him, and

157

Mark's wholehearted, adoring response. All her old suspicions had been true. He did have another woman.

Joey backed away from the door without a sound, fearing her presence would be discovered. When she was out of their view, she turned and hurried back to her car, darted behind the wheel and closed the door.

"What happened?" her mother urgently asked, watching her daughter's quick, but unsteady movements in starting the car and putting it in gear.

Joey waited until she had driven well away from the restaurant and had better control of her emotions before answering. "I saw him with someone else. He was kissing her!" she told her mother in a choked voice. "I guess I won't be marrying him after all!" she added with a hollow, contemptuous sarcasm. "He's just like all the others. Why should a woman trust any man?"

"Now try to be calm, Joey. Tell me again what happened," her mother begged.

Joey's chin quivered. "I went around to the addition and found the entrance. When I looked in, I saw him with a young girl in his arms. She looked like she was used to his attentions—she was hanging all over him. And Mark was encouraging her!" Joey's voice broke and she blinked hard to clear her vision. Tears ran down her cheeks as she finished. "I got away as fast as I could and came back to the car."

"Did he see you?"

"No."

"Then he never had a chance to explain . . ."

Joey looked at her mother as if she had lost her reason. "Explain! Why would I want to hear any explanation? What possible excuse could he have for his behavior? The day after asking me to marry him, I find him in the arms of another woman—or rather, girl," she corrected herself with disdain. "She couldn't be much more than half his age. In fact, I found a picture of her in his van when I was traveling with him. I wondered then . . ."

"But, Joey, I just can't believe this of him," Mrs. Scott said with sincerity. "Isn't it possible this girl could be one of his relatives? People are often affectionate with their relatives."

"A kissing cousin?" Joey said with derisive sarcasm. "No, Mother, this girl was far too beautiful and far too eager to be merely a relative."

"What will you do?"

"Do? Nothing! Never see him again."

"Oh, Joey," her mother said sadly. "Shouldn't you give him a chance to explain himself? I can't believe he would do this to you."

"Mother, this isn't the first time I've been led to doubt him. He's been nothing but a woman chaser from the beginning. If you knew the way he leered at me the first time I saw him! Why, even last night, when he was out with me, he was looking over every other attractive woman in sight."

"Then why did you agree to marry him? You must have sensed something good in him, as your father and I did," her mother asked in a common-sense manner.

Joey was in the midst of turning back onto Highway 1 to return to La Paz and conveniently used the diversion to pretend she was distracted, for she did not know how to answer her mother.

"He . . . he has a way about him," she replied after a few moments. "That's why he's so successful with women. He knows how to delude them, mesmerize them until they don't know if they're coming or going."

Mrs. Scott silently shook her head. "I thought he was so open and straightforward. Are you sure you didn't read more into what you saw than was there?"

"No, Mother," Joey answered in exasperation. "Remember, I've been through this before. Once you find a man who claims to love you in the arms of another woman, it leaves little doubt in your mind."

"Oh, yes—Robin. I had forgotten him," her mother sympathized. "But, you know, I never really liked Robin. The few times I met him I always sensed there was something secretive underneath his engaging manner. I never felt that way about Mark. I thought he was exactly the way he appeared to be—honest and reliable."

The car drew to a halt at the side of the road. Her face crumpling into tears, Joey leaned forward and pressed her forehead against the backs of her hands as they gripped the top of the steering wheel. Her mother leaned over to comfort her.

"For a while, I thought he was, too," Joey cried brokenly, between sobs. "I really believed he was."

Chapter Ten

Joey stood before her bathroom mirror hurriedly pinning her long hair into a plain chignon at the base of her neck. She didn't bother with makeup, not caring that she looked pale and drawn, with dark circles under her eyes from insufficient sleep. She took a quick glance at her watch, tucked her blouse more securely beneath her skirt's waistband, which lately seemed to have increased in circumference, and walked into her small living room.

Her apartment was in disorder, as was usual during the busy season. She had no time to spare for housecleaning, but as she was the only one who saw the mess, she rationalized that it didn't really matter much. Having decided to skip breakfast again, she grabbed her jacket, picked up her heavy, oversized briefcase filled with papers she had brought home the night before, and walked out the door.

In the small apartment building's parking lot, she put the briefcase into the back of her subcompact, which had been restored to working order by the mechanics in Guerrero Negro. It had been ready when she and her parents returned there on their way home from La Paz early in January.

It had been a hasty return. Joey had persuaded her parents to begin their journey home the very next day after the ill-fated trip to Cabo San Lucas. She suspected Mark would come back to La Paz to look for her and took the precaution of leaving the La Playa and staying at a different hotel that last night. Her parents reluctantly came with her to the new hotel, and in that way she erased any possibility of Mark's contacting her by phone or coming that evening in person to find out why she had not shown up. It would have seemed to him that she had simply disappeared.

Since then, Joey learned that he had come looking for her. In fact, Mark had not ceased trying to contact her during the two months she had been back in California. The first phone call came at her office about a week after she had returned. As soon as he had identified himself, she hung the phone up. Then, coming home late that evening after work, she had found her telephone ringing when she walked in and had hurried to pick it up.

"Hello?"

"Joey?"

"Yes . . ." she reluctantly replied, suspicious of the low, male voice. It sounded like Mark, but how could he have obtained her unlisted number?

"Joey, what's going on? And don't hang up! Why didn't you see me at the restaurant?" He waited for an answer, but received none. "I drove all the way back to La Paz that evening and then I found you had checked out of your hotel. What on earth made you leave so fast? Couldn't you have left me word somehow?" There was a long silence over the wire after his barrage of questions. "Joey?"

"How did you get my number?" Joey asked in a strained but cold voice.

A pause before answering indicated his distress at her response. "I found a listing for your father's real estate office and then got his home phone. I called your parents and talked to your mother. She . . . she seemed to indicate you were upset about something, but wouldn't give me any details. She just gave me your number so I could talk to you myself, which is what I intend to do. Now, tell me what's wrong. What's going on?"

Cold as steel, Joey replied, "I don't want to talk to you. Don't call me again."

Quickly she had replaced the receiver, silencing the argumentative low voice protesting her words. How could she discuss her hurt and humiliation with him? How could she bear to hear his inevitable excuses and lies when she told him what she had seen? She still carried the memory of another such confrontation with Robin and couldn't endure the thought of living through a repetition of that scene to have another wretched remembrance to torment her for months and years to come. Her faith in Mark, whom she had loved much more than she had Robin, had been broken. There was no need to make the wound even larger than it already was.

That was the last time she had spoken to Mark, though he had called many more times. On each occasion she had speedily hung up the very instant she recognized his voice. The method seemed to work, for he had ceased trying to call her about a month ago.

However, it was only a short time later that he had attempted to see her. She was working on an audit one Sunday afternoon at the desk in her bedroom. Something made her glance out her second-story window, which overlooked her building's parking lot, and she caught a glimpse of a tall, dark-haired man, looking very much like Mark Chavira, moving just out of sight toward the building. In another moment her doorbell was ringing. Nervously she paced back and forth while she listened to it ring a dozen or more times. After several minutes she saw him walking back to his car with what seemed to be angry strides. With widened, watchful eyes she observed him, a mixture of feelings churning in her heart—fear, anger, and a hurt sort of wistfulness. If he loved her so little as to be untrue to her, why couldn't he leave her alone?

For the past three weeks, however, it seemed her desperate wish had come true. There were no more phone calls or attempted visits. Even her parents, whom she had stopped seeing at dinner because they continually made unwelcome suggestions that she was being unfair to Mark, seemed to have finally given up trying.

When Joey had stopped coming by for supper, Mrs. Scott had taken to calling her almost every evening. In spite of the fact that her daughter was still angry with her for giving Mark her phone number, Mrs. Scott continued to take his part, urging Joey to at least allow him to explain, even to give him another chance. Joey began to suspect that Mark was keeping contact with her parents, particularly her mother, and was managing to bend her already softened heart in his direction. On one occasion Mrs. Scott had tried valiantly to coax Joey to come to dinner on a particular night, arguing that they hadn't seen enough of her lately. Joey had steadfastly declined, claiming her heavy workload as an excuse, for she feared if she went to her parents' house that evening she would find the table set for four instead of three.

But finally it seemed even her mother had lost hope for remedying the situation, and for the past two weeks or so Joey had enjoyed a semblance of peace. At last she could concentrate more fully on her work and meeting her deadlines. If only she could sleep better at night, she would be fine, she had lately told herself. If only she didn't dream of Mark so often, think of him, remember his arms about her . . . only to remember those same arms embracing someone else.

Never again would she let her heart be captured by a man, she had decided with certainty and determination. She would forever remain her own woman—independent, unattached, self-sufficient.

She got into her small car, its marred front end having been cosmetically improved at a body shop, and drove about fifteen minutes to the two-story office building in Los Angeles which housed Layton and Brook Accountancy Corporation, along with several other small businesses.

After greeting the receptionist and one of her co-workers, she walked to her cubbyhole office and laid her heavy briefcase on the gray carpet, already cluttered with files, reference books, and papers. She threw her suit jacket onto one of the wooden chairs placed in the small room and sat down behind her well-used, but serviceable, wooden desk. She turned the desk calendar to the current day, March 16.

"Hi, Jo! How's it going?" asked Thomas Brook, the firm's junior partner, who popped in to see her. He was a tall man, overweight, with red-blond hair now beginning to turn gray as he entered his late forties.

"Hello, Tom. Pretty good," Joey replied, always glad to chat with Tom Brook. He was invariably pleasant and easygoing, unlike the firm's senior partner and founder, Harlan Layton—or Mr. Layton as he preferred to be called.

"How's the Springfield Foods account coming?"

"I finished it last night," she replied, bending over to drag her briefcase next to her chair so she could reach the file he had asked about.

"Great! I'll look it over then. Good work, Jo! Looks like we can make our deadline for that after all. You must have been up most of the night," he said, taking the thick pile of papers from her hands.

"Until about two thirty, but I don't mind. I'm glad to get it out of the way."

"Just because it's the busy season doesn't mean you have to kill yourself, you know. You've been looking awfully dragged out since you got back from Mexico."

"She's gotten skinnier, too," said Chris Langley, the firm's newest accountant, who suddenly appeared at her door. He was a young man, just out of college, with moderate good looks and a cocky, irreverent disposition. "She used to be pretty foxy looking, but the last couple of months she's just gone down the drain."

"Thanks, Chris," Joey replied, unperturbed. It was of no consequence to her what he or any other man thought of her appearance.

"She's just tired from working so hard—a feeling which you've probably never experienced," Tom remarked half-seriously to Chris.

"You're right about that," Chris quipped light-heartedly before breezing off down the hall.

"I don't know about that kid," Tom said, shaking his head. "I thought he would have settled down by now. Well, take it easy, okay, Jo?"

"Sure," she said with a smile as he left her office.

Take it easy! She didn't want to take it easy. It was better to bury herself in work than to think or feel or remember. Someday, when enough time had passed, she would be cured. But until then, the only answer was work.

Her determined thoughts were broken into by the sound of her name being called excitedly from down the hall.

"Jo! Jo! You here?" Suddenly Mr. Layton appeared at her door. He was a short man, very thin, with iron-gray hair, whose normally pale complexion was now bright-

166

ened with agitation. "Come into my office, Jo," he said, motioning quickly.

Immediately she rose and followed him to his large office at the end of the short hall, wondering all the while what on earth was causing such a commotion. He directed her to sit in the leather chair opposite his desk as he closed the door behind them.

"Great news, Jo!" he said, almost out of breath. "I just got a call from Sunrise Development Company. They want us to take over their account—immediately! I guess they're not satisfied with their old accounting firm, didn't say just why. Anyway, they specifically insisted that you be in charge of it."

"Why?" she asked, totally at a loss.

"I don't know," he said, spreading his hands in the air. "You had one account last year in Orange County. Maybe they heard of you by word of mouth."

"Orange County . . ." Joey said, her voice dropping as the company's name suddenly began to ring an ominous bell in her head.

"Yes!" he said impatiently. "Haven't you heard of Sunrise Development Company? It's the biggest and most prosperous one in that whole county, maybe even the state! What a windfall! I've been waiting for twenty-five years for a well-known company to hire us. Just think of the prestige it'll bring, being able to mention their name as one of our clients. We'll probably be able to raise our rates, expand. Think of the new business we can attract!"

Joey's heart was beginning to pound, but she tried to remain calm. "Who was it that called you?"

"Mark Chavira himself!" Mr. Layton replied triumphantly.

Feeling the blood draining from her face, she suddenly felt faint and grasped the arms of her chair.

"You all right?" Layton asked gruffly. "Tom keeps telling me you're working too hard. Here, take a sip of this coffee," he said, pushing a half-full Styrofoam cup across the desk.

Weakly she leaned forward and took it, fighting hard to regain her composure. She had to get herself out of this somehow.

"Since it's such an important client, wouldn't it be better to put someone more experienced on the job?" she asked, trying to keep her voice steady.

"Ordinarily I would—I'd take it myself—but Chavira insisted it should be you. In fact, he said it had to be you, or we didn't get the account. You must have made a good impression somewhere along the way for people to recommend you so highly. Not that I'm surprised. You've been doing a fine job for us, Jo. I wouldn't worry about not being able to handle it. If you have any problems, just ask me. Oh, and don't think you won't be rewarded for this. I'm seeing to it that you get an immediate raise."

"W-what about my other clients?" she asked, clinging with hope to the only remaining objection she could think of. "I don't think I have time for a new account."

"Oh, listen, don't worry about that," he said with a sweep of his hand. "I'll reassign some of your work. You can spend all the time you need on Sunrise. I don't want anything to interfere with your work on *that* account . . ."

His phone rang, and she was glad to have some time to ponder while he was involved in conversation. Why wouldn't Mark leave her alone? He had his other woman. Why should he continue to pursue her? It must be clear to him by now that she no longer wanted his attentions. Oh, what difference did it make what his motivation was? Now he almost had her cornered! It was unthinkable to have to see Mark again, much less to have to work for him. Her heart could not stand to confront him with his fickleness, to reveal her own humiliation, and to listen to his inevitable false explanations. She must keep her dignity this time. She must not fall into his trap. Besides, if she saw Mark again, if she allowed him the opportunity to talk to her, to make advances . . . she feared she might believe his lies.

She must find a way out now, and quickly! She could tell Mr. Layton what had happened between her and Mark, embarrassing though it would be. But thinking that over for a moment, she decided that Layton would probably not be very sympathetic. Sympathy was not in his nature, but greed was. He coveted that account and wouldn't let a young woman's romantic problems stand in the way. If she refused to take the job, she would very likely get fired.

She could quit and try to get a position elsewhere, but what would be the use of resorting to such an extreme measure if Mark was willing to go to these lengths to reach her? It was certainly not for business reasons that he had recruited a small, little-known L.A. accounting firm, in the middle of the tax season, to take over his company's work. Well acquainted with his tenacity, she knew he would catch up with her sooner or later. Meanwhile she would be in the position of a fugitive, always on edge and never knowing when she would be found and pursued again. Maybe it *was* best to face him now and have it out with him, so that he would never again come after her. Was there any easier solution?

Mr. Layton was finishing up his conversation. Thinking quickly, Joey asked as he put down the receiver, "Do you think I could have someone working with me on the Sunrise account? Maybe Chris, or one of the others?"

It would be an advantage not to be alone, she reasoned. Another person around would necessarily buffer any exchanges between her and Mark. Also, if she were lucky, she could ask the person working under her direction to take over the brunt of the work, thereby making it unnecessary for her to go to Mark's office very often, that is, if Mark still wanted her company's services after their initial meeting. But, judging by past experience, he probably would; he was not one to give up in a day. He would probably hold her to her work obligations so he could have several weeks to deal with her.

"Maybe," Layton replied thoughtfully. "Chris would be the only one I could send—the others are just too busy. Even he has the Friedenburger account that he's got to finish by the end of the week. If he makes good progress on that, I suppose I could arrange for him to work with you. Would that make you feel better?"

"Yes," she breathed, relaxing a bit. "When do I have to go out to Sunrise?"

"I said you'd be there the day after tomorrow."

"I see," she whispered, taken aback by how soon she'd have to see Mark again.

"He asked for that day specifically, because he'll have some time in the afternoon to go over the books with you. Apparently he's got a tight schedule."

"I'll be there then," she said, managing to smile. Layton's last statement gave her some cause for relief. If Mark was away from his office a great deal, it made it even less likely that she would see him often, especially if she could have Chris to take over the work. In fact, if she were fortunate, she might have to see him only once, at the first meeting. Perhaps she could muster enough stamina to steel herself for one confrontation.

The remainder of that day and the next passed much more quickly than Joey would have liked. When the day came that she had to go out to the Sunrise Development Company, she still felt mentally unprepared to see Mark again. She had hoped that somehow she could have pulled

170

herself together, so that she could meet him with cool self-possession. Instead she had become increasingly nervous, eating very little and sleeping less.

She came to work that morning wearing a tailored, but unadorned, tan suit and a cream-colored blouse with an open collar. Her hair was severely pinned back in the style she had lately been wearing.

"You look terrible today, Jo. Are you feeling all right?" Tom asked with concern when he came into her office shortly after she arrived.

"Oh, I'm okay," she said, trying to hide her jitters.

"You look awfully pale and your hands are trembling. Have you taken your temperature? Maybe you're coming down with the flu."

"No, I don't think I'm sick," she assured him. "I just had a little trouble sleeping last night."

"Nervous about going out to that big new account?" he asked with a smile.

"Well . . . yes."

"Don't worry, you'll do a fine job. Don't let their prestige scare you. It's just another company."

"Okay," she replied with a gentle grin, knowing he was not aware of the true reason for her state of nerves. "Is Chris in yet? Mr. Layton told him to try to finish the Friedenburger account so he could go out to Sunrise with me this afternoon."

"No, not yet. He's not noted for his punctuality, you know."

"I just hope he finished. I . . . I'd like to have some moral support when I go out to Sunrise," she said, forcing a smile.

"From Chris? I hope you're not *that* desperate!"

"Did I hear my name being bandied about?"

Joey looked up to see Chris poking his head into her

office. Relief immediately began to replace the tension showing in her face.

"Speak of the devil!" said Tom. "On time again today. That's three days in a row—a new record!"

"Chris . . ." Joey began, but was beaten to the punch by the young man she was addressing.

"Did you see the big basketball game last night on TV?" he asked Tom with great enthusiasm.

"I just turned it on for the last few minutes. I was too busy to watch any more than that," Tom replied.

"Oh, you missed all the best plays, then," Chris told him with a dismissive wave of his hand. "What a game! I never saw anything like it," he continued, enraptured, and drew Tom out of Joey's office toward the coffee machine in the hall.

Almost dying of nervous impatience, she sat at her desk and listened as Chris gave Tom a lengthy play-by-play account outside her door. When he finally finished, a full ten minutes later, the two men parted and went to their separate offices. Releasing a sigh of pent-up emotion, Joey quickly got up and walked to Chris's office, a tiny room similar to hers.

"Chris," she said, almost holding her breath, "did you finish the Friedenburger account?"

For a second he looked at her blankly. Then, as light dawned in his eyes, he said offhandedly, "No, still working on it, Jo."

The floor seemed to give way beneath her. "But Mr. Layton asked you to have it done by today so you could go with me to Sunrise."

"He said to try to have it done. I didn't get the impression he was particularly concerned. Why do you need me on that job anyway?"

"So you didn't even try?" she asked in an angry panic, ignoring his question.

"Jo, the big game was on last night," he explained calmly. "I wouldn't miss that come hell or high water."

"How much more work do you have to do on the account?" she asked, hoping she wasn't reaching for straws. "Could you finish it this morning?"

"No way. I have to see another client in half an hour."

"Couldn't you postpone your appointment to finish it? Wouldn't you like to have the experience of working on a prestigious client like Sunrise?" she asked.

"And have to drive all the way to Orange County day after day? No thanks! Now that we have that one, we'll be drawing other big accounts. I'll wait for one that's closer," he said complacently.

"You may not be around that long!" she silently retorted, furious at his careless attitude. Saying no more, she turned and rushed back to her own office, shutting the door behind her. Leaning against the doorframe, she pressed the palms of her hands to her face and let the tears of nervous frustration flow. Her last bastion of protection was taken away. Now she would have to see Mark alone.

In a moment, she tore her hands from her face. "Oh, what difference does it make?" she asked herself, suddenly angry over the whole situation. Mark was just another man, wasn't he? She had managed to deal with him before on her own. Surely she was capable of handling this. She shouldn't allow herself to be turned into a sliver of quivering gelatin by any man!

Her newly regained determination managed to hold through the morning and into the noon hour, when she was on the freeway driving southward to Newport Beach in Orange County. But as she approached a tall, sparkling new office building near a fashionable and elegant-looking shopping mall, her nerve began to fail again.

Jitters returning, she left her car in the parking area and walked into the lobby of the building. A coldness came

173

over her when she saw Sunrise Development Company listed on the lobby directory, and her stomach was feeling queasy even before she got into the elevator.

She stepped out onto the designated floor and walked down the hall, her heart pounding with the thought that she might run into Mark at any moment, until she came to the door of the Sunrise Development Company's office suite. Below the stylishly lettered name was a modern design representing a sunrise. It seemed like a prophetic symbol, only to Joey's mind it looked more like a sunset. Almost sick with apprehension, but knowing there was no other choice, she opened the door with an icy hand and walked in.

"Hello, may I help you?" asked a pleasant young woman of about Joey's age sitting at a desk directly inside.

"I'm Josepha Scott from Layton and Brook Accountancy."

"Oh, yes!" she replied with an instant smile. "We've been expecting you. Come this way, please." She rose to her feet and walked toward a closed door.

Joey stood as if frozen in the middle of the room.

"Mr. Chavira will be in later, but he asked me to have you use his office for today," the secretary explained, casually turning toward Joey as she reached the door.

The information that Mark would not be behind the closed door was the only thing that enabled Joey to move to catch up with the young woman. The unmarked door opened into a large office dominated by a huge desk of beautifully finished hardwood. There were floor-to-ceiling windows behind long, loose-weave drapes on two sides of the rectangular room, allowing bright sunlight to permeate the spacious office. In one corner was a scale model of a shopping center enclosed in glass. On the walls, which were covered in textured beige cloth to harmonize with the plush, burnt-orange carpeting, were a number of artist's renderings of various new buildings and shopping centers. A comfortable couch and two easy chairs were arranged around a low coffee table.

The secretary pulled up an orange-brown leather chair to the front of the large, tablelike desk. "He suggested you could work here. I'll go and tell Mrs. Tolliver, our comptroller, that you've arrived."

The young woman left, silently closing the door behind her. The polite smile on Joey's face quickly faded. She sat alone in the handsomely furnished room, almost feeling Mark's presence. Her eyes drifted to the high back leather chair on the opposite side of the desk. How long before Mark would be sitting there, staring back at her with his dark, probing eyes, asking why she had left La Paz so suddenly?

All at once the door opened and she jumped. Her frantic eyes turned toward whoever was entering.

"Hello, I'm Hilda Tolliver," said a brown-haired, well-dressed woman of about forty-five who came into the room carrying a pile of papers. "You're from Layton and Brook?"

"Yes, Josepha Scott," she replied, nervously rising and extending her hand.

"It's very nice to meet you," the poised, friendly woman said, briefly shaking Joey's hand after she had set the papers on the desk. "I've brought in our general ledger, the construction ledger, and our last financial statement and tax return for you to look over. If you'll have a seat, I'll start briefing you on our company and our current construction projects," she said, pulling up a second chair to the desk. "Would you like some coffee?"

The next hour or so was spent covering all financial aspects of the firm's business. "Is there anything I haven't mentioned that you have a question about?" Mrs. Tolliver asked when their conversation was about to conclude.

"Yes," Joey said hesitantly, her heart beginning to beat faster. "Was there any particular reason why your company switched accounting firms? So far I haven't had any indication that the previous firm mishandled your books."

Mrs. Tolliver smiled. "That's a good question! I thought they had been doing an adequate job. I guess Mark had had a few minor disagreements with them, but nothing serious. It seemed very odd to change at this time of year, too, when all the CPA firms are so swamped with work. But Mark came in one morning a few days ago, said we were going to change accountants, and that was that. He looked so determined, I wasn't about to argue with him."

She glanced at Joey as if conscious that she may have sounded disloyal. "Don't get me wrong, Mark Chavira is a wonderful boss, but lately . . . well, he's been a little edgy. He went down to Baja California over Christmas to pick up his mother, and ever since he got back he's been rather morose. None of us on the staff knows why as yet. We're afraid perhaps his mother is ill or something. I thought I'd mention it in case he seems strangely out of humor for such a successful young man. It's only a temporary thing, I hope."

"His mother was in Baja?" Joey asked breathlessly, forgetting herself in the shock of this new revelation.

"Yes, I believe she has relatives there. He drives her down to stay with them for several weeks at a time about twice a year. She's a widow now, and likes to keep in touch with her remaining family. Well, I'll leave you to look over the books. Mark should be back in a while. He's out at a ground-breaking ceremony. Let me know if you have any questions."

"Thank you," Joey said absently as the other woman left the room. So, perhaps the old lady Ted had referred to actually was Mark's mother. Maybe she had been wrong in assuming that the woman he traveled with was the young, dark-haired girl in the photograph. Confused, Joey leaned forward to rest her elbows on the desk and buried her face in her hands. Had she been wrong about everything?

A moment passed, then she took her hands from her face and sat back in the chair, attempting to calmly put everything into perspective. No, she couldn't have been that wrong about his character. She may have been mistaken about the identity of the woman with whom he traveled in his van, but she had caught him embracing the young girl. He probably renewed his romance with her during each visit he made to his relatives accompanying his mother. No, this new piece of information changed nothing. He was still the womanizer who had chased after her through Baja California, and nothing altered the fact that he had lied when he told her he had no other woman. He was still a man she did not want in her life.

Her mind settled once again about that question, she straightened up and began shuffling through the papers on the desk in front of her. She might as well get to work, ridiculous though this situation was. She wondered how long it would take before she was angrily dismissed. If he was still pursuing her, that was inevitably what would happen, for she would certainly reject him again after listening to his lame excuses.

But perhaps he would make her stay on to punish her with abusive words and torment her with his armchair psychology. How would she endure it? How hateful he was to put her through this! Somehow she must find the resources within herself to fight him.

The minutes passed slowly as she leafed through the papers with clammy hands and icy fingertips. It was impossible to concentrate and her eyes did not want to focus on the columns of figures laid out in front of her. Three o'clock came and went, then three thirty, and still he had not come. She began to hope that he would not come at all.

It was nearing four o'clock when her ears picked up the sound of a male voice outside the door.

"Is the accountant here?" was his sharp question.

"Yes, she's in your office," was the secretary's barely audible reply.

Joey instantly grew petrified. There was a short silence and then the door swung open. All at once she saw Mark Chavira's dark eyes staring down at her, his expression grim and watchful. Quaking within, her mouth dry as cotton, she nevertheless found her eyes being drawn magnetically to his.

The long weeks of separation seemed to slip away in the few fleeting moments they gazed at one another, and now it was as if she had left La Paz only yesterday. Time had done little to alter the deep emotions that lay between them.

The door closed. Saying nothing, he strode over to his desk and sat down across from her in the big leather chair. Leaning back, he continued to study her, his eyes hard and clear—almost omniscient.

Joey's mind grew foggy as she searched the familiar face which continually haunted her thoughts, waking and sleeping. It was more gaunt now. He seemed tired, no longer quite the carefree, self-possessed man she had known. But his gray three-piece suit and necktie did nothing to subdue his rugged appearance, his compelling masculinity.

His eyes still on her, he took in a slow, deep breath and exhaled it softly. "You're hard won, Joey," he told her in a quiet voice.

She dropped her eyes, taking in his words with a shudder.

"I almost wouldn't have recognized you," he went on. "Have you been ill?"

She shook her head negatively, unable now to meet his eyes.

"It can't be that you've been pining away for me," he said, a hint of sarcasm to his tone.

"No," she replied, finding her voice. "Why have you brought me here?" she asked, wanting to get the issue over with quickly.

"Why have you come?" he countered.

"I had to or lose my job!"

"Yes, I thought it would be that way," he said, smiling to himself.

"Why did you go through all this trouble to get me here?" she asked, her voice cold, but cracking with tenseness and anxiety.

He regarded her intently. "Obviously because I had to see you again. We're getting married, remember? I want to know why you left La Paz without a word and why you've been avoiding me ever since. I had to devise some way to keep you near me for a while, so I'd have a chance to get you to explain yourself. This was the only way, short of kidnapping you."

She kept her eyes lowered, studying her tightly clenched hands in her lap. "I'm not marrying you."

"Why not?" he calmly asked.

Her lips trembled but her voice was now firm. "Because I did come to see you that day at Cabo San Lucas. Only I got there early—hours before you were expecting me— and I found you kissing some young girl. You lied to me," she accused, raising her reddened eyes to his. "You told me there was no one else. I should have known that wasn't true. I found a picture of her by accident in your van."

Mark stoically nodded his head. "Yes, that's what your mother said you believed."

179

"My mother! I thought you had managed to get her on your side," she said bitterly.

"I was desperate, Joey. I had to get information from somewhere. Don't be angry with her. She thought she was doing it for your own good."

"You've probably mesmerized her into believing you're innocent the way you do every other woman," she said with scorn.

"Maybe I am innocent, Joey. Did that ever occur to you? Or are you so afraid of marriage, you'll believe anything to avoid it?"

"I saw her in your arms, Mark! What else can I believe?"

Chavira gave a short sigh and reached into his coat pocket. He withdrew an envelope, opened it, and took out a small pile of color snapshots. Rising from his chair, he walked around the desk and sat down in the chair Mrs. Tolliver had used. "I'd like you to look at these," he said, handing her the pictures.

Reluctantly she took them, taking particular care not to touch his hand in doing so. Looking through the snapshots, she saw they were pictures taken at a wedding and reception. Mark was in some of them.

"Do you recognize the bride?" he asked.

She looked closely at a couple of the pictures. The bride was a lovely young girl, slender, with long black hair. "It's the girl I saw you with," she said very softly, feelings of both relief and agitation welling up within.

"Yes. She's Carmelita, one of my cousins. I've known her since she was born. That letter with the picture you apparently came across was one she had written telling of her wedding plans and inviting my mother and me to come. The picture had been taken at her engagement. My mother wanted to help with the preparations, so I drove her down there late in November. I went down again myself around Christmas, as you know, to stay for the wedding and take my mother home again."

Joey was suddenly beginning to feel foolish, but she asked stubbornly, "Why were you kissing her?"

He sighed and smiled. "Mexican people are very affectionate. You could find that out for yourself if you'd relax a little," he said with an amused glint in his eye. "Your mother told me you arrived about ten thirty. I think that was probably about the time I was telling Carmelita that I would give her and her new husband a honeymoon trip to California as a wedding present. She was very happy about that."

"You've had a lot of time to think up that excuse," Joey weakly protested.

"Joey, if you like we can drive down to Cabo this weekend and you can ask her and her husband about it yourself," he said convincingly. "I'm sure she'd be happy to assure you that she is in fact my cousin and that there never was anything out of the ordinary about our relationship. In fact I imagine she'd find it all rather amusing, your thinking that she was in love with me. She's very young, just turned eighteen, and she's always seemed to regard me as a confirmed old bachelor. Every time I see her she needles me about not being married yet, and now she ribs me that she's beaten me to the altar."

He paused and studied Joey's downcast expression. "Well, would you like to go down to Cabo and question her this weekend?"

Joey's reply was barely a whisper. "No."

"You believe me then?"

Reluctantly she nodded her head.

He made a light chuckle. "How come you're so depressed? Because this means you'll have to marry me after all? You thought you had found a means of escape and now you're caught again! Is that it?"

181

She shifted uneasily. "No . . ." she answered lamely.

"No? Why did you just run away without at least asking me for an explanation about what you saw?"

"Because I . . . I didn't think you could possibly have any. I was hurt. I just wanted to get away."

"Get away. That's what you've been trying to do ever since I met you. Your mother told me you were very nervous that morning about having accepted my marriage proposal. You've been eager to believe the worst about me all along."

"I had good reason," Joey protested.

"Good reason!" Mark objected with amused outrage. "What good reason?"

"Many reasons. For example that conversation I overheard between you and Ted in the restaurant. I realize now that the old lady he was so tactlessly referring to was your mother, but at the time I somehow had the impression that he was talking about some young woman you were having an affair with. Since Ted seemed to look upon you—even admire you—as a womanizer, that was naturally what I assumed. Besides, he thought you were after me."

"Well, I was after you. He was right about that. But you see, because I'm a bachelor Ted likes to think that I have all kinds of fun that he thinks he's missing. And if you ever spend any time talking to him, I'm sure you'd soon realize he isn't enough in touch with the younger generation to know their interpretation of the term old lady. Does that clear up your doubts?"

"Well, I suppose it settles that question, but there were other things. Like . . . like the first time I saw you in Ensenada. The way you looked me over, and right after I had seen you eyeing that redhead. Why shouldn't I have concluded that you were a skirt chaser?"

"You mean at the gas station? How did I look at you?"

"Exactly the same way you looked at the redhead."

He sighed patiently. "I don't even remember a redhead, Joey. How did I look at you? What did you find so intolerable about my behavior?"

Joey was incensed. "Why, you . . . you leered at me! Like you wanted to seduce me!"

Mark was thoughtful for a moment and a nostalgic smile slowly came over his face. "Yes, I remember now. You practically stripped your gears trying to get out of there. Underneath that bold, indignant stance was just a scared little girl. I thought you were so adorable, I memorized your license number as you were driving away. I would have found you again one way or another even if we hadn't met on the road."

Joey swallowed hard, feeling her destiny being sealed. "But answer my question. Why did you look at me like that?" she asked earnestly. "That's why I had a bad opinion of you from the very beginning."

He narrowed his eyes at her. "It seems I remember now your trying to pin me down on this once before."

She nodded. "At dinner in San Quintin."

"And my answer wasn't satisfactory?"

"No. You just said there was nothing wrong with a man admiring a beautiful woman."

"Well, is there?"

"You men don't understand what it's like to be treated like a sex object! It's degrading," she said, some of her old fire returning.

"Now hold on a minute," he said, reaching to close his fingers about her wrist. "Let's analyze this calmly, shall we? I was standing there at the gas station and I noticed you checking your tires . . ."

"And you were leering at me," she interjected, conscious of the warmth of his fingers on her skin, but not attempting to extricate herself from their grasp.

He pondered a moment. "I was admiring you, but I don't think I was leering—not yet."

"You seemed more intrigued with my anatomy than anything else," she pointed out.

He let go of her wrist, and she found she was disappointed at the loss of physical contact. She began to sense where her heart would lead her, whatever his explanation, and, surprisingly, she felt a warm relaxation stealing over her.

Mark leaned back in his chair, casually crossing his arms over his vest. "Well," he answered, "you do have a beautiful figure, you know. As a man, was I expected not to notice? Maybe I just happened to be looking at the wrong place when you turned around. I assure you I had noted your lovely face—those intelligent, innocent eyes, the turned-up nose, the flawless complexion."

Joey pretended to be dubious. "Okay, let's say you were admiring me. Then I gave you an indignant look."

"Imperious might be a better word, like I was trespassing on hallowed ground. It just served as bait. I had to see what such a fascinating creature would do under stronger provocation, so I gave you a genuine leer. Your expression turned even more venomous. It became an amusing challenge, then, so I tried the old come-on look I used on girls when I was sixteen. It never worked then either, now that I think of it. Anyway, you panicked and drove off." He looked at her with sadness and amusement. "And you've been afraid of me ever since."

Joey gazed down at her lap and said nothing.

"Any other complaints?" he asked, after a few moments.

"Yes. The underhanded way you got me here," she replied with a slightly provocative pout.

"Well, Joey, you hung up on me every time I tried to call you. And you wouldn't see me. You were home that

Sunday I came over; I saw your car in the parking lot. You just didn't answer the doorbell, did you?"

Joey silently acknowledged the truth of his statement.

"I thought so. What was I to do? I had to devise some way to get you in a situation where you couldn't escape me. One time when I was talking with your mother over the phone, I asked her what your boss was like. When she described him from things you had told her, I suspected he was just the type to help me, unwittingly, to set up a trap. I suppose it was a little deceitful to hire your firm just to get you here, but I do intend to keep your company's services. Besides, you've been pretty tricky yourself, with all these maneuvers to escape me."

Joey veiled her eyes with her lashes, not knowing what to say. Mark was right, of course, but she was reluctant to admit it. In a moment she realized she was under the scrutiny of his studious gaze.

"What is this ridiculous hair style?" he said, his narrowed, displeased eyes moving over her plain coiffure. He rose from his seat and squatted beside her, as if to get a closer look. "I'm surprised you didn't put one of those thick black hairnets over the whole thing," he muttered.

An involuntary smile crept over Joey's lips. All at once she felt his hands attacking the mound of hair at the base of her head. "Mark, what are you doing?" she asked, raising her hands protectively towards her head.

"Getting rid of this monstrosity," he replied, unexpertly pulling out hairpins and throwing them onto the desk. Soon her long silky hair came loose and fell softly about her shoulders. "There. That's more like the Joey I used to know," he said, looking over his work.

Kneeling beside her chair, he leaned forward and gently kissed her lips. If she had hoped she would be impervious to his touch, she wasn't. She began to feel jittery again, but it was a pleasant nervousness. When he kissed her a second time, she found herself responding, returning the pressure of his lips. She could feel a rosy warmth filling the cold void in her body, bringing her alive again. When he drew away, he looked into a lovely face, no longer pale with strain and fatigue, but radiant and glowing with love.

"Joey, you missed me, didn't you? Say you missed me," he ardently whispered.

"I missed you," she admitted in a tiny voice, her hands entwined at the back of his neck.

"You told me once you'd marry me. Tell me again—now," he urged.

"Oh, Mark," she murmured, turning her face away, "please don't rush me."

"I have to, or we'll never see our wedding day." He shifted himself in front of her so he could look into her troubled eyes. "Still afraid you don't know what you'd be getting into?"

She nodded her head.

"Come on, then," he said, taking her gently by the hand and rising to his feet. "Let's sit back here on the couch and talk about it." With hesitance she got up and followed him to the comfortable sofa at the other side of the room. When they were settled next to each other on the soft cushions, he said, "Now let's see if I can paint a picture of what our married life would be like." He thought a moment. "First of all you'd come and live at my house . . ."

"And I'd have to take care of all the bedrooms, bathrooms, living rooms . . ."

"Joey," he interrupted, "how do you think they get taken care of now? I have a cleaning woman, a gardener, and a part-time cook. There's no reason for me to dismiss them just because you move in. You won't have to do any housework, if you don't want to."

"Really?" she said, not quite believing him.

"Well, I don't like to brag, but if it'll help my cause, I am a fairly wealthy man, you know."

"Maybe I wouldn't fit into your social circles," she said, seizing onto a new objection she hadn't thought of before.

"My social circles include people like Ted, so I don't think you need to worry about being outclassed. That was a silly comment," he said, reaching up to tweak her nose. "Okay, so you'd live at my house. I know you like your career, so you can continue working if you like, though you'd probably have to change firms after we're married—conflict of interest, you know. Maybe you'd want one closer to home anyway. Or, if you don't want to work at an outside job, you can work with me."

He leaned toward her and placed a hand on her shoulder. "That's the beautiful part of this relationship, Joey. My work takes up most of my life. But you understand business and can share my interests, even give me advice. Do you know when I first was positive you were the girl for me?"

She shook her head.

"When we were on the road and you mentally converted kilometers into miles without batting an eyelash. I said to myself, 'I need this beautiful human calculator around when my investors come up with questions about their future profits.' You could be such an asset to me . . ."

"You just want me for my business expertise?" she whined, pretending to be offended.

"Only during the day," he assured her, breaking into a grin. "At night I'll need you for other things."

"Like what?" she innocently asked.

He gave her a knowing look, almost repeating the leer she had so despised when she first saw him. She didn't mind it this time, however. In fact, it made her heart beat faster. It seemed he sensed her quickening pulse and he gathered her into his arms, pressing her strongly against

187

him. Eagerly she accepted and returned his warm, ardent kisses. Now she knew how foolish she had been to run away from his love all these weeks. In his arms was where she belonged.

"Don't you see how wonderful it could be?" he said softly, some long moments later as he leaned back, still holding her close. "We'd make a perfect team—in the office and in the bedroom."

His low voice crept into her ear along with his steady heartbeat as she rested her head against his chest, feeling secure in the strong arms about her. It seemed all her fears and misgivings had finally vanished.

"How about it, then. Will you marry me?" he asked.

"I will, Mark. I'd be a fool if I didn't," she replied, blinking back tears of joy. "I've been too much of a fool already," she added, nestling her cheek against his vest.

As if still uncertain, he asked, "Is there anything else that worries you? Anything more you want?"

She lifted her head and looked up into his handsome face. "Yes, this," she whispered, reaching up to pull his head down toward hers. Pressing herself against him, she kissed him wholeheartedly, then urgently.

"All right, young lady," he said, pulling his lips from hers and holding her away from him slightly. He looked with amusement into her disappointed eyes. "You'll just have to wait until we're married for more." He smiled at her dumbfounded expression. "You know the old saying, Joey. 'A farmer won't buy the cow if he can get the milk for free.' "

She looked at him, puzzled. "That's what mothers used to tell their daughters."

"With women so independent these days, it might be a wise adage for men to follow. I'm afraid you still may become skittish and start putting me off about setting the date. So, until the wedding band is safely on your finger, you can't have anything more than a brief good-night kiss."

She looked at him with dejected eyes. "How soon can we get married?"

"I was hoping you'd ask! How about the second Saturday next month?"

Her eyes grew suspicious. "Why did you pick that date?"

"I happened to have called a few churches in the area, and that was the earliest opening I could get."

"That's only three or four weeks from now!"

"You won't have to exist on good-night kisses for long," he pointed out. "We can use one of the new restaurants I've built for the reception. One of my tenants in the last shopping center I developed runs a bridal shop, and she said she could arrange for a gown for you on short notice. All we have to do is get the blood tests and marriage license."

"You must have been awfully sure of yourself to have planned all this!"

"One of us has to think positively," he said with innocence.

She grew distressed. "In La Paz you said you wouldn't be a domineering husband. Now you're making plans without . . ."

"I won't be domineering, I promise. You'd never let me get away with it, even if I tried," he said, giving a lock of her hair a gentle tug. "But you haven't been around lately, so I took advantage of what was probably my last opportunity to have a free hand. I have to get you to the altar somehow. I looked a long time before I found you. I'm not going to let you escape now. We've already had too many close calls. So let's just set the date for next month and get it over with. Once that hurdle is behind you, I think you'll find yourself a very happy Mrs. Chavira. Okay?"

She took a deep breath. "Okay," she acquiesced, sensing he was right, as always. It was time to trust her heart, and Mark.

Apparently forgetting his words about farmers and free milk, he rewarded her for her correct answer with a very long, very lingering kiss.

LORI HERTER

For more information
visit:

LORI HERTER

For more information
visit: www.speakingvolumes.us